Edge of the Known Bus Line

Edge of the Known Bus Line

James R. Gapinski

Etchings Press

This publication is made possible by funding provided by the Shaneen College of Arts and Sciences and the English Department of the University of Indianapolis. Special thanks to Ingram Spark and to those students who judged, edited, designed, and published this novella: Spencer Martin and Jessica Marvel.

UNIVERSITY *of*
INDIANAPOLIS

Published by Etchings Press
1400 E. Hanna Ave
Indianapolis, Indiana 46227
All rights reserved.

blogs.uindy.edu/etchings/
www.uindy.edu/cas/english

Printed by Ingram Spark
www.ingramspark.com

Printed in the United States of America

ISBN 13: 978-0-9988976-0-8

First Printing, 2018

Colophon: Main Text: Baskerville, Title Text: Optima

Chapter 1

The bus pulls into my stop on schedule with *Out of Service* on the marquee. It's packed with the familiar workday crowd—nameless commuters recognizable by their smells and propensity to encroach on my legroom. So I assume that the marquee is a simple mistake. I sit in my usual seat—one of the few that isn't stained with coffee, piss, puke, or miscellaneous—and I settle in for the forty-minute ride. I'm bored and not particularly happy, but that's typical of six o'clock in the morning. I take out my compact and put on some mascara. It's smudgy, but it's not like it matters anyway—last week, I had lipstick on my teeth half the goddamn day before a customer said anything. When you work at a deli, most people ignore you. They're just so grateful that the number on their little paper slip has been called. They press their faces against the glass and ogle the meats. If they happen to look up or make small-talk, I usually scare them off by chopping up fresh, bloody slab in front of them.

The bus proceeds through its usual route making its usual stops. The teenager with bad BO gets off first, the cripple who uses his cane as a surrogate groping mechanism gets off second, and the guy who always stares at my cleavage gets off third. Same as always. The stops roll on, people exiting as the line winds down. There are just three passengers left now—four if you count me. But just before sliding into Seattle's Belltown neighborhood, the bus makes an abrupt turn down a side street. The bus veers again, jerking into a tight alleyway. I call out "Is this the right way?"

The bus driver taps the sign above his head: *Please Do Not Disturb Driver*. Graffiti swishes past the windows; a few close shaves send sparks off the bus. Several maneuvers later, and the bus pops out of the winding alleyway, gliding onto a tree-lined road that I don't recognize. I look at the college student who stares at my ass and the relatively polite guy who reads the paper each day. Both of them shrug. The woman who naps until the end of the line is napping, true to form, and it doesn't occur to me that I should wake her.

Newspaper-Guy gets up and says "Excuse me, where are we going?"

"Sit down!" yells Bus-Driver. Newspaper-Guy complies. Napping-Woman stirs at the booming voice but doesn't get up.

"We gotta do something. This isn't the right way," says Ass-Starer. Newspaper-Guy hushes him.

Napping-Woman finally blinks and stretches, sitting up in her seat. "Hey, this isn't Belltown. Where are we?" she asks.

"I don't know," I say.

"Hey, driver, where are we going?" asks Napping-Woman. Bus-Driver taps the sign again. "Hell no! Where are we?" Napping-Woman insists, rising from her seat.

Bus-Driver holds up a chromed handgun. Napping-Woman sits back down. The passengers exchange looks and formulate whispered plans to overtake the bus. They ask me to lead the charge. Apparently they can all brainstorm the stupidly simplistic plan, but they are too chickenshit to actually storm the gun-toting lunatic themselves. Needless to say, I don't comply—I'm not dying today. I survived a shitty childhood and an asshole husband; I'm not about run directly at some nut with a handgun. The passengers bicker but eventually settle into their seats. Newspaper-Guy pulls the cord to request a stop.

The bus continues into a tunnel. The massive underground passageway continues for hours, headlights barely penetrating the void. Napping-Woman actually takes another nap as we drive in the endless dark. The sun has almost completely vanished when the bus emerges. In the dusk, a sign reads *Welcome to Out of Service*, complete with a wispy *S* on *Service*, accenting the previous words with its yellow underscore. Underneath, *Population: 66* is written in drippy paint. Add a third six and you've got the intro to a cheesy horror movie.

"You've got to be kidding me," Ass-Starer says.

The entire town consists of shanties and one broken down bus with flat tires, shattered windows, and lots of oxidization—it's really more like a giant bus-shaped slab of rust than an actual bus. There's a huge flaming barrel in the center of town, and a group of disheveled people are gathered around it. More people emerge from shanties as the bus grinds to a halt with that low hissing sound characteristic of all buses. The accordion door opens. "End of the line," Bus-Driver says.

"This ain't right," mumbles Ass-Starer.

9

"Everybody off," Bus-Driver reiterates, his hand on the gun again.

I go first. I'm still not dying today. I can catch the next bus out. Bus-Driver hasn't pointed the gun at me yet, and I want to keep it that way. I actually give a nod and smile as I exit, partially out of habit, and partially because I don't want a bullet in me. He is letting us off. I take it as a gift.

The three other passengers file out behind me. A semicircle of grimy people gawk at us. Apparently nobody bathes in Out of Service. They approach and inspect us, reaching out and tugging at the hems of our clothes. I swat away the pinching fingers. Newspaper-Guy thwaps a nearby groper with his rolled-up reading material.

"You're not wearing heels," one of the crowd finally says, her eyes dropping to my loafers. The woman is dressed in an old seat cushion, gutted and split open across the zippered side. The edges of her makeshift garment are sutured with wire. I don't engage the woman. Her observation annoys me. Who the hell wears heels to work on a Tuesday morning? I'm not gearing up for a gala event with black ties and evening gowns.

"Heels are better. They make nice shivs. You can kill just about anything with a stiletto," she informs me.

"It's okay," a man with a traffic cone on his head remarks. "Her blouse will make a nice net. Maybe we can catch some fish."

"Wait just a minute," I say. "Nobody's taking my blouse."

"There aren't any fish left. That stream's gone to shit," a man butts in, ignoring my objection. His chest is smeared with mud, as if that makes a suitable shirt, and he wears a loincloth made from woven bits of what appears to be dental floss. Attached to his extension cord belt is a white bag full of spark plugs. On the front of the bag is an anthropomorphic tooth cartoon, and the caption reads *Don't forget to smile today!* I want to have a dark laugh but can't force one out.

I ask "What the hell is this place?

"Can't you read?" A man near the back holds up a length of pipe, motioning toward the town's welcome sign.

A naked little boy scampers toward Napping-Woman. He is missing one entire hand, and the other hand only has two fingers left. Naked-Boy grabs her purse and picks at the contents, pinching the objects between his thumb and ring finger, steadying the rest of the bag with his wrist-nub. Napping-Woman drops the sweater from her other hand and backs away from the boy. I think the kid freaks her out.

Napping-Woman moves toward the idling bus in a pseudo-moonwalk. She jams her arm in the door as it tries to slam shut. She slides through the door and groans, pushing her weight against the metal contraption that's desperately trying to lock her out. Naked-Boy drops the purse and gasps. The townspeople stop their ambient mumbling and hold perfectly still, watching the woman pushing through the door. The hush gives the moment an anticipatory vibe. Looking at these pallid surroundings, I decide that any anticipation must be the anticipation of bad things to come. I shout "come back!" to Napping-Woman. Before she can wiggle through the door in either direction, there's a loud *bang* and a glob of brain matter spits out, splattering the boy. Bus-Driver repeats "fuck, shit, dammit," over and over, ending with "I hate this route."

There is a chugging sound and a gurgle of exhaust, and the bus drives off with Napping-Woman's dead body still wedged in the door. Her mouth hangs open in the breeze, unhinged from the gunshot's stippling. The floppy tongue drips more goopy reddish blobs. Newspaper-Guy holds back vomit and Ass-Starer just stands there. My ears ring, but beyond that I'm fine—I guess ruptured brain matter should shock me, but it doesn't. I've seen gore like this before. What do armchair shrinks call it? Desensitized?

Naked-Boy starts to cry, and a woman wearing a blue plastic tarp rushes over. She uses the tarp's hem to dry the child's face, but the nonabsorbent, slick material doesn't do much other than spread the blood around. Some part of me wants to scold this urchin for rooting through Napping-Woman's purse, but another part feels like I should help. Kids aren't supposed to get sprayed with blood—that seems pretty fucking obvious, even to somebody like me. I bend down and offer my cardigan.

"Thank you," Tarp-Woman says. We tear the cardigan into two pieces, despite somebody yelling that the garment is too useful to rip. We each work on a different part of the boy. She mattes the blood from his hair, and I gob up the brain matter on his face. The boy's sobs devolve into whimpers.

"I'm sorry everybody's so grabby," Tarp-Woman says. I don't respond. I'm sure she is sorry, but the fact remains that these grubby, half-starved people are talking about dividing up my clothes. Tarp-Woman continues to explain: "It's just that we rely on new people and passing buses for provisions. The townspeople will be disappointed that the driver sped off so fast. Usually, the driver drops off any stuff that gets left on the bus. Eyeglasses, magazines, leftover food. You know, regular bus stuff."

I glance at the townspeople as they pester Newspaper-Guy and Ass-Starer, rifling through their meager possessions as if the entire town's saving grace could appear in somebody's wallet. "Will they be angry?" I ask.

"The townspeople? Probably not. It depends on what faction you join, I guess."

"What do you mean?" I ask.

Tarp-Woman laughs and places the blood-drenched cardigan scrap into an empty Breyers ice cream container for safe keeping. I hold my piece out at arm's length; it's covered in equal parts dirt and blood, turning the whole cardigan into a sopping brownish thing. "Honey, you don't get it yet, do you?" she asks after her chuckle subsides. "They aren't going to hurt you. You're one of us now." Her smile reveals yellow teeth and bleeding, gingivitis-ridden gums.

"Don't forget to smile today," I say, and I join her sick laughter. What the hell is wrong with me? This place is a shithole.

My possessions are scavenged within minutes—apparently most of the cosmetics from my purse are useful accelerants, and they'll make it easier to keep the fire barrel lit for the next few weeks. Tarp-Woman explains that the barrel is the center of everything. It gets cold at night, and people often sleep around the barrel in one large heap rather than in their shanties. It's also used for cooking, and it's a main source of light—apparently it's overcast all day long. I'm willing to give up my cosmetics as long as this coven of dirty people doesn't come after my blouse.

Tarp-Woman introduces herself. I don't want to know her name, so I continue to tell myself that her name is Tarp-Woman. I want to distance myself from this place and its people. I'm just here until the next bus rolls in. I grew up on a farm, and I know that giving things names is dangerous business. I never named our pigs. Never. Once, my sister accidentally named a pig, and she accidentally told me about it, and I purposefully told our mom. Mom made my sister slaughter Named-Pig, and then my sister had to eat pork, bacon, or ham for every meal until Named-Pig was gone.

Naked-Boy is Tarp-Woman's son. He has a name too. "How old is he?" I ask because this is a standard question about children.

"He's seven. I'm sorry that he started going through that

woman's purse. He doesn't know any better. He was born here, about a year after I arrived."

"You've been here eight years?"

"Yes, eight years. Some people don't last long, but I met my boyfriend within the first week. He showed me how to survive." Tarp-Woman retrieves the cloth from her Breyers container and twits the cardigan, squeezing its contents into a hubcap. She bobs her head as she works, like some grotesque version of a housekeeper wringing out the laundry.

I try to process this information. Not only have people been living in this shithole shantytown for years, but they are bringing new life into the world here. This is no place to raise a child. I've been in this so-called town for a few minutes and I know that. "Does anybody try to leave?" I ask.

"Of course, people try. They go in, and they promise to get the others when they've found the exit, but they never make it back." She motions to the black-hole-esque tunnel that consumed the bus moments earlier. "Well, I suppose that's not entirely true. One group made it back. Just once, though. It was a search party, looking for the bodies of the last group. They were supposed to go as far into the tunnel as they could in a single day, then turn around and report what they found. Only half of the search party returned. They were several days overdue, starving, and covered in sores. They got separated from the others in the dark. They died a few days later. Nothing we could do for them."

Most of the townspeople move back to their places around the fire, taking Ass-Starer and Newspaper-Guy with them. They pat the pair on the back and laugh—perhaps it's newcomer orientation, but I'm thankful that the group is content to leave me with Tarp-Woman. She puts away one cardigan scrap and works on the next. Naked-Boy watches the blood pooling in the hubcap. He reaches to dip a finger into it, but Tarp-Woman smacks the top of his two-fingered hand.

"What about the bus? It knows how to get through the tunnel. Does it ever pick up passengers?" I ask.

Tarp-Woman laughs again. Her laugh is shrill and crackly, like a cartoon witch. "Sometimes. The one that drops off passengers never does."

"But there's another bus? One that comes for pick-ups?"

"Well, it's usually the same bus. It just depends on whether it's starting the route or ending it. But even when it picks up, the bus doesn't go anywhere." She smacks the boy's hand away a second time.

"What do you mean?"

"The bus marquee always says *Out of Service* as its final destination. Whenever a bus comes in, it picks up passengers, drives them into the tunnel, and then drives back out a few hours later. No other stops. It just takes you right back where you started."

"That can't be."

"Well, honey, it is." Tarp-Woman drops the wrung-out scrap

back in the container and prods the bits of gray brain matter in the hubcap with her fingernail. Her nail is long and beginning to arc into itself, like a stunted version of those *Guinness Book of World Records* nails that seem to spiral forever.

Tarp-Woman hands the hubcap to Naked-Boy. "Go cook it in the fire barrel" she instructs. He walks without lifting his feet, sliding each one across the dirt so as to avoid any major bumps as he carries the delicate, sloshing prize. A little bit drips from the side, and he freezes in panic. "That's okay, honey. Keep going. Just be careful. And make sure you cook it long enough. Don't eat any until the blood boils, okay?"

"Okay, mama."

"Barely anything in there anyway," Tarp-Woman mutters. "I really wish more meat had come out. That speck will hardly feed anybody." She smiles with those rotten teeth again. "Who knows though, maybe the bus will drop her entire body off on its next pass through."

Chapter 2

I wake near a pile of emaciated townspeople. It's fucked up. It's like waking from a nightmare only to get catapulted back into some shittier nightmare. I think it's daytime, but it's hard to tell. It's overcast and gray. It's like this place is such a shithole that the sun doesn't even want anything to do with it. I must've inched closer to the heap of townies throughout the night without realizing it, desperate for the fire barrel's warmth. Their legs twitch in their sleep. As they writhe around, their clothing makes jingling and rustling sounds—garments sutured with paperclips and twine come loose in the night, and half of them are nude. I push away the nearest woman, freeing myself from this heap of grimy people. She grunts and rolls over, but she does not wake. In her sleep, the woman rubs her elbows against themselves. I think she has psoriasis.

Ass-Starer is slumbering face-down in the pile. If I'm going to get out of here, maybe the other bus passengers can help me. Despite Tarp-Woman's insistence that the route goes nowhere, I decide that I still have no choice. I must see for myself; I must study the circular bus route to see if there are hints of another exit somewhere in the tunnel. Once I see the tunnel more clearly, I can plan my next move. I hate Ass-Starer, but he should be equally motivated to leave, and I can shelve my anger to combine our escape efforts.

I nudge Ass-Starer a with my foot. "Hey, wake up," I say. When he does not move, I pick up dirt clumps, and I drop the clumps on the back of his head until he stirs. He mumbles "What the fuck?" and rolls over.

"I should ask you the same thing. What the fuck?" I say, motioning toward his chest. His shirt is stained with some cryptic insignia—a circle with a dot in the middle. His jeans are torn off at the knee, and the coarse scraps are used as a headband. His cheekbones are streaked with mud, like those black lines that athletes put under their eyes. The rest of his skin is ashen from the fire barrel's smoke.

Ass-Starer stands up and tries to brush some lingering dirt clumps off his head. The dirt doesn't come off. It just smears around and mattes down his hair. He yawns and stretches. His back cracks—I think he's too young to have back issues, but I guess sleeping on a pile of people will do that. "It's a Chicago Faction initiation rite. This is their symbol," he finally replies, explaining the insignia while failing to mention how the rest of his clothing got tattered to hell in one day's time.

"Their symbol is a doughnut?"

"It's an eyeball," he says, double-checking the stain on his shirt to be certain. He's like a kid trying to explain a shitty drawing to a parent, giving a description of what it's supposed to look like, despite the fact that it looks zero-percent like an eyeball. "Have you joined a faction yet?" he asks.

"No, I don't want to do that," I say. I've heard whispers of this faction bullshit from Tarp-Woman. I have no interest in learning the particulars.

"What do you mean? You have to join a faction. If you're not a follower of the Chicago Faction or the Pittsburg Faction, then you can't stay in Out of Service," Ass-Starer says.

I lose it and scream "Are you shitting me? We've been here for one fucking day! You can't even handle basic social etiquette enough to keep your eyes off my ass, but somehow you have the entire caste system of Out of Service figured out, complete with rank and file obedience, in one goddamn day. You little shit!"

As I berate Ass-Starer, he actually leans to one side, craning his neck to get a look at my ass. So I punch him in his muddy face. "Where is Newspaper-Guy!" I demand, making sure to spit on him a little as I shout. If Newspaper-Guy is still sane, then maybe I can convince him to board the bus with me, and we can decipher the tunnel route together.

Ass-Starer points to a shanty behind us. I walk over and pull back a used painter's drop-cloth. The drop-cloth is supported by a rusted rain gutter, two pieces of PVC pipe, a few crumbling tree branches, and the ever-present hallmarks of this place: mud, dirt, and muddy dirt. I don't find Newspaper-Guy inside this haggard shanty. Instead, there's a naked, emaciated man sleeping face-down. His back is riddled scar tissue—a mound of bubbly, hardened skin forms little gyres of discoloration across the surface. I bend down and see that each scar is a faint letter or word, and dug into the hump is a fresh wound. This wound barely bleeds. His back is already so mangled that the veins

21

have probably collapsed and receded—I wonder how his flesh isn't already gangrenous. The fresh injury forms a headline, and I understand why Ass-Starer didn't want clarification when I asked for Newspaper-Guy rather than using a real name. Apparently, to people living in Out of Service, this guy's back is the newspaper. The current edition reads *Chicago Faction Welcomes Two New Members; Mysterious Woman's Allegiance Still Unknown.*

I lose it again. "What the fuck purpose does this serve? You guys have cardboard and tarps and other shit you can write on. What the fuck!" I scream at Scarred-Back. He wakes but doesn't look startled. I punch the side of his head. Nothing gives, like punching a wall. I want to keep hitting him, but I know I shouldn't. I think about the headline. "Newspaper-Guy has joined a faction now, hasn't he?" I ask, calming myself and sitting down next to Scarred-Back.

"I'm Newspaper-Guy," he replies, evidently unconcerned with the fact that I just beat him. He sits up and extends his hand. There is a beetle between his pinky and ring-finger. I shake his hand. The beetle gets squished and oozes some yellowy guts.

"I don't mean you," I explain. "I mean the guy who came with me. The older one. He always read the newspaper on the bus."

"Oh," Scarred-Back says. "Is that what I'm reporting this morning? They just etch the news into me. I don't really get to see it."

I almost laugh, but I don't. There isn't anything funny about this. "Do you have any cigarettes?" I ask.

"No. Wish I did." He reaches his spindly arm around his back; he scratches the fresh wound and digs his fingernails into the older scars. As he probes his scars, I roll up my blouse sleeve and feel the hardened scar tissue on my wrists—a couple years old at this point. The wobbly slash marks are seemingly insignificant compared to this man's wounds. I normally cover them up with bracelets and long-sleeved shirts, but in this fucked up place nobody will notice.

"How long have you been here?" I ask.

He shrugs. "Don't really know. Long time."

"Have you ever tried to take the bus out?"

He shakes his head. "No. Never bothered. The bus doesn't go anywhere. It's a loop," he says, mirroring Tarp-Woman's warning from yesterday. He twirls his finger in the air to illustrate the loop.

"Sorry I hit you," I mumble.

He doesn't say anything but looks confused. Maybe this guy is so accustomed to daily pain that the assault barely registered.

I go back outside and sit near the center of town, where the bus pulled up yesterday. There is a piece of cement in the ground with a broken bit of metal sticking out. I think it used to be a bus stop sign. I pace around the vestigial pole and keep my vigil.

Tarp-Woman is awake now. She's tilling the earth with a plastic dust pan, using it like a trowel. She does not plant anything. Instead, she pulls things out of the ground: rocks, roots, and a few animal bones. Naked-Boy gnaws on the roots, scraping away bits of dirt and bark, grinding the thing to a point with his teeth. Tarp-Woman gives her pile of dirty stones to a nearby man. The man is missing an eye. He has fashioned an eyepatch out of a Trojan condom wrapper. The wrapper seems like a terrible choice to me, but I commend the decision to cover the empty eye socket rather than letting it fester. All the other townies seem to have at least one unattended injury that looks terribly infected—I don't know how they're still walking around. This place is a cauldron of bubbling pus and blood and mucus. An entire swimming pool of rubbing alcohol wouldn't be enough to sterilize this shithole.

Condom-Eye runs toward a group of rats and throws rocks at them. He misses and mutters something to himself. I think he is hunting—I wonder why Condom-Eye doesn't collect rocks while leaving the hunting to Tarp-Woman or somebody else with depth perception. Tarp-Woman smiles at me and asks me about factions. I shake my head and say "No, I don't want to join a faction." She accepts my refusal and continues to harvest rocks. Condom-Eye finally hits a rat. The rat starts to move slower, like it's messed-up but not quite dead. Naked-Boy runs over to the wiggling creature and stabs it with a root. He licks the rat's tail and smiles. He's about to take a bite when Tarp-

Woman scolds "No, honey. Not until it's cooked."

I roll up my slacks. I try to keep the hem out of the mud. The longer I sit and wait for the bus, the deeper I sink into the mud. I change positions. I find several patches of solid, dry ground. Within fifteen minutes, these hardened surfaces always reveal themselves to be illusions, and I sink again. There's no way to escape the filth of this place.

The bus does not come. As the day drags on, more townies approach and ask me to join a faction. There are two meek elevator pitches for the Pittsburg Faction, but most of the day involves an endless barrage of impassioned speeches about the Chicago Faction. The followers each interpret their beliefs a little differently. Some tell me that they're required to pray daily at the Cubs Shrine—it's basically an oversized foam finger from a Chicago Cubs game that's been skewered on a stick. Others tell me that the Cubs are blasphemous, and they pray to a ratty old White Sox T-shirt. Regardless of these minor details, the overall message remains the same. They all agree that a miracle bus with *Chicago/O'Hare* on the marquee will arrive any day now. The foretold bus will whisk them away to a promised land flowing with milk and honey and barbeque ribs. After they finish living the high life in Chicago, they'll continue to the O'Hare airport. Then they'll fly around the world, feasting and rejoicing and basking in the sun on tropical beaches.

They encourage me to learn more about their religion at the hotel—that's what they call the broken-down bus in the center

25

of town. The hotel doesn't rent rooms. It's basically Chicago-Prophet's mansion. Somebody tells me that Pittsburg-Prophet used to live there, but he died a couple years ago, and only a few people still follow the dead man's teachings. I don't give any indication that I am listening to this bullshit. I hope that if I ignore these townies, they will leave. I retain this stoicism for several hours, then one of them grabs my shoulder, urging me toward the hotel. I lose it and punch her stomach. "Don't touch me!" I scream directly into her ear. "I don't want to join your batshit religion. I'm getting the fuck out of here as soon as possible!"

The woman scampers off. When she's at a safe distance, she calls out "It's not a religion. It's a philosophy."

Tarp-Woman approaches a few hours later, and I worry that she will make another attempt to enlist me. Instead, she introduces me to Condom-Eye. He is her boyfriend and Naked-Boy's father. "He is an excellent hunter," Tarp-Woman says. "I couldn't go on without him." He looks embarrassed and bashful. He asks me some questions, the kind that neighbors ask when welcoming somebody new. But the questions are all in past tense, as if to remind me that my old life is dead and gone. I answer bluntly and keep my eyes trained on the black-hole-esque tunnel, hoping the bus will arrive soon.

"Did you have any pets?"

"Once."

"Where did you work?"

"Deli."

"Were you married?"

"Once."

"Did you have any children?"

I do not answer this last question. Condom-Eye gets the hint and leaves.

I think it's almost sundown—things are getting a bit darker and grayer now. The bus still hasn't come. It's looking more and more likely that I'll be here for a little while. I decide that I'll need a nighttime plan that does not involve sleeping around that stupid fire barrel. I want to remove myself from this town and its people.

I find some dry-ish ground on the outskirts of town, far enough from the shanties that nobody will wrongly presume I've joined a faction. I spread out my meager belongings on a burnt log, and I take inventory. The townspeople have left me with eyeliner, credit cards, the straps from my pillaged purse, and an empty tube of ChapStick. I also have the items I'm wearing: shoes, slacks, blouse, bra, and panties. I plan on keeping these items intact, especially the slacks and blouse. I will not wear seat cushions or tarps as clothing—and there's no goddamn way that anything of mine will be used for their fishing nets.

Tarp-Woman notices me sitting alone, inspecting my scant possessions. She walks over and offers to give back the ripped cardigan, still bloodied and sitting in her ice cream container. I tell her to keep it. "No, you'll need it," she says. "You can use it

27

to strain the river water. Boil the water before you drink it." She hands me a charred soda can already half full of water.

She also offers me some rat meat. I accept the gift. I haven't eaten anything all day, and my stomach roars at the sight of something remotely edible. I presume it's revolting, but I'm starved, and I eat so fast that it's down my throat before even registering a flavor on my taste buds. She leaves me with a raggedy satchel that contains some dried-up beetles. "For tomorrow," she says. "They're not so bad. Just crack the carapace and eat the insides. Like a lobster or crab."

"Thank you," I whisper. This is not a phrase I am accustomed to. Normally, if somebody does something nice for me, they have an ulterior motive, and I tell them to go fuck themselves. Maybe this is true of Tarp-Woman too, but I can't afford to alienate my only ally in this shithole.

My stomach gurgles and fights against the rancid meat. I take a stroll around the shantytown's exterior. All around Out of Service, ashen trees twist skyward. Beyond that, there are hills. Above the hills, mountainous crags slice the blackened clouds. I have zero experience mountain climbing, but if the bus turns out to be a bust, I will need to explore this rocky barrier for a way out.

I collect wood from the burnt forest and start a small pile on my chosen patch of dirt. Finding suitable firewood takes longer than expected; most of the wood disintegrates in my hands, brittle and almost ethereal. In the burnt forest, I find other trinkets—a broken watch, soggy bits of cardboard, a pile of guitar picks, a muddy dish sponge. I spy a few more items deeper into the woods, on the base of the hills. Maybe this stuff was placed there by the citizens of Out of Service in some weird ritual. It seems too far away from the center of town to be random litter. I do not bother with any of the trinkets for now because the fire is more important. Deeper into the hills, there are totems or signposts of some kind—I can't quite tell what they are from a distance. The wind whips up, bringing dust and soot and urgency with it. I cover my face with my hands, and I make my way back to my patch of dirt on the outskirts.

I watch the sky for signs of stars or a moon. There is nothing but cloud cover and the whistle of cold, unforgiving wind. If I don't keep track of the time, I know the days and nights will blend together. I use my eyeliner to mark two tallies on the underside of my blouse: one for today, one for yesterday.

I inspect my haul. The area is caked in mud, but I manage to spark a fire using the brittle bits of dry wood. I curl my body around the embers to keep warm. Before I fall asleep, some shithead comes over to ask me about factions again. I throw a rock at him. I miss, but he gets the idea and heads back to town.

Maybe there is some protection afforded by joining a faction. Maybe it's technically a smart idea. But it's also a tacit way of agreeing to the rules of this fucked up society—a way of resigning to live here indefinitely. I don't want to be a citizen of Out of Service. I want out. I will sleep by myself near my own insignificant fire on the edge of town, and I will make sure my hygiene is a fraction better than everybody else's—this will be my silent rebellion.

Chapter 3

The bus pulls into town with Napping-Woman still wedged in the door. Her dangling foot doesn't quite touch the ground as the bus idles, but the flesh probably grazed the pavement on sharp curves in the tunnel. Napping-Woman's toes are ground down to rounded bumps, sticky with coagulated blood. I wonder if Bus-Driver stayed on the bus for forty-eight straight hours. He couldn't have left without dislodging the corpse. The bus is one of the older models without a rear exit.

Bus-Driver opens the door and pushes out the body. It's got a terrible smell, like skunk and shit mixed with a hint of blood. He also dumps out an empty computer bag, a half-eaten PB&J sandwich, and a brick—as if a piece of masonry ever helped anybody survive in a shithole shantytown. The townspeople are surprisingly civil about who gets to eat the PB&J—perhaps I underestimate the merits of their society, or perhaps they are all eyeing the bigger, meaty prize. The brick is taken into the ashen forest, toward the hills.

I try to board the empty bus, but Bus-Driver demands a ticket. I only have my expired one from two days earlier. I try to haggle over the nonnegotiable fare, and he pulls the gun. It's a moot point anyway—even if he lowers the price, I don't have a single penny on me. Somehow, in my ongoing bus vigil, I hadn't planned on a fare—why the fuck is he charging for a circular loop anyway?

I back away from the bus but ask one last thing: "Do you

live on the bus?" After I say it, I realize it sounds like a dumbshit question that a kid might ask. Bus-Driver shakes his head and chuckles. If he left the bus at the end of his shift, that means he must've removed the body. So that also means he must've stuck it back in the door before driving out to this middle-of-nowhere Out of Service shithole shantytown.

Bus-Driver yells "all aboard for Out of Service," like he's a turn of the century train conductor or some bullshit. The empty bus exits. I hurry around the shantytown looking for Tarp-Woman. Maybe she knows what happened to the money from my purse. I hope they didn't use the dollar bills as fuel for the fire barrel, like they did with Newspaper-Guy's paper. If I can get some money before the bus returns, I can hitch a ride out.

I do not find Tarp-Woman, but I do find money scattered all over the camp, mostly near the rusted bus stop remnant. When purses, wallets, and pockets are ripped open for provisions, the change is immediately discarded. Naked-Boy helps me— maybe he thinks it's a game. Tarp-Woman finally returns from an unsuccessful rat hunt with Condom-Eye, and she gives me an empty Folgers tin to keep my change in. When I'm finished, I look almost as filthy as the other townspeople, but I get more than enough for a bus ticket. Most of it is in nickels. I count out exact change and save the rest.

The bus rolls back a few hours later and opens the doors to let phantom passengers exit. Bus-Driver even says "no shoving," perhaps out of habit.

I try to board the bus. I hold the exact change in my cupped hands like an offering. Bus-Driver shakes his head and says "I'm dropping off, not picking up. You'll have to wait for the next one."

"Are you fucking serious?" I scream.

Bus-Driver twists his body to show me the chromed handgun is still tucked into his waistband. I calm down and back away. I'm not dying today. The doors close. The bus rolls out of town, into the tunnel. I run after the bus, thinking that maybe I can follow its brake lights through the void, leading me to freedom. Before I even reach the tunnel, the bus speeds up and the lights are sucked into the tunnel's nothingness. I take a few steps into the darkness. Behind me, I can hardly see the town. The gray sky is so choked and muted that it barely offers a beacon. With another few steps, I'll be in total darkness. I remember Tarp-Woman's stories about search parties that never came back from the tunnel. I back-step slowly, returning to a bastardized version of safety. I sit on a rock near my collection of burnt sticks. I keep my eyes locked on the tunnel, knowing that it could spit out a new bus at any time. Or it could suck me up and squish my organs, compressing me to a singularity like the black hole that it is. I count my change while I wait. I brush off as much dirt and ash as possible. I try to remain clean and calm and optimistic. I'm getting the fuck out of here.

"You're wanted at the hotel," a teenager with no teeth

tells me, pointing to the broken, rust-coated bus in the center of town. She licks her gums. She tries to crack her knuckles to look intimidating. Toothless-Teen tries again and again, but she fails to make a convincing crunching sound. She winces as the sores on her fingertips burst open. I think one of her blackened fingernails actually falls off in the attempt.

"Why?" I demand.

Toothless-Teen shrugs. Two large men approach, flanking the teen and sufficiently making up for the lack of knuckle cracking. They are soon joined by another dozen people. They are all carrying homemade weapons with varying degrees of deadliness. The flail made from cat toys doesn't bother me, but I worry about the nail gun. The gun doesn't have an air compressor and can't actually shoot, but it's blunt and heavy and could do some damage as a bludgeon. Ass-Starer is there, that little shit, and he's got a broken Miller Lite bottle—simple and elegant, a glass bottle can shred a face quick. This is starting to look like a mob, and I know I must comply or face their wrath.

"Alright, let's go. But there's no way I'm going to be one of his concubines," I say.

"Don't flatter yourself," a woman says. She's missing chunks of her hair. Her scalp is raw, a bright red visible through the crusty dirt encircling her entire body.

The mob waits outside of the hotel. The accordion door is missing. Inside, one guard holds a spear. The spear's tip is a thick shard of something—I think part of a terracotta pot fastened to a pole with an iPod charge-cable. Another guard holds a club-like thing caked with grime. I can't tell what the club is made of. For practical purposes, it's just a monolithic mass of dried dirt.

Chicago-Prophet is at the back of the bus. All the bus seats are ripped out, but long bolts stick out of the floor marking their former places. Most of the bolts are jagged and rusted—I bet half the people here have tetanus. Chicago-Prophet's throne is made from a disconnected toilet. There is a hole cut in the floor of the bus, and there's a bucket underneath the toilet. I think Condom-Eye is responsible for emptying the hotel's sewage each day. Either he is slacking off, or Chicago-Prophet shits a lot—there's a rank smell and dung beetles crawl around everywhere. Granted, everybody here subsists on a wholly carnivorous diet, and it messes with the digestive tract. Chicago-Prophet wears a raccoon skin cloak. His body isn't as emaciated as many of the other townspeople—the benefits of being in charge. He's holding a double-barrel, big-ass sawed-off shotgun. As far as I can tell, it's the only gun in the entire town. I ponder scenarios for how the shotgun ended up here. What kind of nut brings a shotgun onto a city bus?

I kneel before him. I hate this, but it feels like when I faced Bus-Driver's handgun. I whisper my mantra to myself: "I'm not dying today."

"Please, get up. I know you don't really want to kneel," Chicago-Prophet says. I rise. I don't like that he called me out on the fake sign of respect. "I hear you've been making trouble," he says.

"Like what?" I honestly don't think I've been making trouble.

"Like abusing residents," he explains. "We're a nonviolent society."

I want to say *Nonviolent? Are you shitting me?* I consider the people I punched—Ass-Starer who seems ready to use that broken bottle, Scarred-Back with his gouged flesh, and some cult follower eager to please a shotgun-wielding psycho. Napping-Woman is the only actual death I've witnessed here, but this place exudes violence, seeping from every dirty pore and dismembered limb. Instead of these objections, I say "I'm just having trouble adjusting. I'll keep to myself from now on." On some level, this is the truth. I want nothing to do with Out of Service—I won't bother the residents if they don't bother me.

"Speaking of adjustment periods, I hear you haven't aligned with the Chicago Faction yet," Chicago-Prophet says.

"No, I haven't."

"So you're part of the Pittsburg Faction?"

"No," I reply.

"Well you can't be a member of the Cleveland Faction. Those people don't even live in town. They keep to the hills, and their prophet is crazy." Chicago-Prophet has a disarming calmness to his voice. I feel less threatened than when I first entered the hotel. It almost seems like he is concerned for my well-being—the prodigal soul, lost without a faction.

"I'm not a member of any faction," I say. "I just find it a little hard to believe that some bus with *Chicago/O'Hare* on the marquee is going to show up and save everybody." Chicago-Prophet writhes on his throne for a moment, and to avoid escalation I add a belated "with all due respect."

Chicago-Prophet thinks for a moment or perhaps pauses to create the illusion of thinking. "The Chicago bus won't rescue everybody. Just the followers of the Chicago Faction," he says.

"Either way, I don't believe it. I don't want to make waves. I just want to be left alone."

"There are always nonbelievers when newcomers first arrive. But you'll come around. They always do." I nod as if to agree, even though I have no intention of ever coming around. "If you're part of a faction, you'll last longer here. The other Chicago Faction members will look out for you. We're a community," he says.

I consider Tarp-Woman's kindness. She explained things to me on the first day. Her son helped me collect change, and she gave me that Folgers tin. She gave me food and a means to collect water. I wouldn't have survived without her so far. Sure, I helped wipe off Naked-Boy after he got coated in Napping-Woman's blood, but Tarp-Woman has been talking to me and helping me beyond any sort of reciprocal obligation. Maybe Tarp-Woman thinks we're friends? And what happens if

Chicago-Prophet orders her to stop helping me?

But I can't join a faction. I remind myself that I'm not staying. I'm just passing through. I'm getting the fuck out of here. I shake my head at Chicago-Prophet and think for a minute. I don't owe this nut job anything. I want to tell him to fuck off, but he's still holding that big-ass shotgun, so I'm polite. "I can't join a faction. It's just—" I try to think of a more illustrative way to explain it to him, but nothing comes.

"Okay," Chicago-Prophet says. "But we've got more business to discuss."

"Oh?"

"I hear you're a butcher," he says.

"Sort of. I work in a deli. We don't do all of the cuts on-site, but some," I explain. "I also grew up on a farm. I know my way around a pig carcass."

"Excellent! I've got a proposal for you," he says. "You don't need to join the Chicago Faction, but I'd like an alliance."

"An alliance?"

"Or you could think of yourself as an independent contractor. A freelance butcher," he offers.

"So you want me to chop up those shitty rats?"

"Well, I wouldn't put it quite like that, but yes. My followers kill whatever animals they can find, but they don't know how to butcher them properly. They leave a lot of the meat on the bone, and they're constantly rupturing the organs, which creates a lot of contamination issues. Food poisoning is a basically a way of life here. The prep is just messy. We would just roast the rats whole, but there are so many diseased bits. It's problematic. We really need them cut up. We could use your help."

"And what do I get out of it?"

"You'll get a small cut from each animal. Let's say that you can keep a twentieth of whatever you butcher."

I think about this. Making an alliance is a slippery slope—it renders me an active part of their shithole community. However, this is my third day, and I already missed one opportunity to get on that bus. Townie banter warns that the bus could take days, even weeks during slow seasons. There's no way of knowing how long I'll be stuck here. I need to make sure I survive until the next bus—or the next few buses, depending on how long it takes to map the route. I don't need to pray to a Chicago Cubs foam finger, but who am I to turn down a mutually beneficial arrangement like this? I ask for details: "How often?"

"Probably once a week," he says. "Basically, whenever we have fresh meat."

I want to laugh at this—there is no such thing as fresh meat in this place. "Okay. But I want more than a twentieth. I'll do it for a tenth of the meat," I say.

"Fifteenth," Chicago-Prophet counters.

"Twelfth."

"Deal."

"So you just wanted me to join the Chicago Faction so I'd butcher for free, didn't you?" I say, caught up in the haggling and momentarily forgetting the power dynamic.

"No," he says. He sets the shotgun down, leaning it against his toilet throne. It's a meaningless gesture since there are still guards posted nearby, but I appreciate the attempt at civility. This place is such a shithole that any measure of decorum is like Prince Charming himself rode up and offered a bouquet of two-dozen goddamn roses. "How about this? You can keep a tenth of the meat if you come to the hotel and listen to my teachings. Whenever you take your cut, you come hear a sermon."

"No other conditions? Just come listen to some proselytizing, and I get extra food?"

"That's the deal. I really think you'll come around when you hear my teachings. It has nothing to do with free labor."

"Okay," I say.

When I leave the hotel, a pile of carcasses is already stacked up near my pile of burnt wood, eyeliner, empty ChapStick, credit cards, Folgers Tin, and burnt soda can. There's a cleaver and paring knife wedged into the top of the bloody pile.

The carcasses are sickly things. They are covered in sores and engorged ticks. I push aside the small animals and find Napping-Woman's leg at the bottom of the pile—I know it's hers because the toes are ground to the bone. I'm guessing they already half-assedly butchered the rest of the corpse before Chicago-Prophet summoned me to the hotel. I cut the best I can. The diseased flesh is difficult to work with, and the rats are tricky even with the small paring knife. And I must admit that I'm distracted—I keep looking up from my work to check on the bus stop. I cut everything as if it were a pig—and raccoon, rat, raven, and human cuts are very different from pigs. I'm not sure if my butchery is turning out any better than the townie amateurs. Toothless-Teen comes over with a bathroom scale. The display is partially cracked, but it still seems to work well enough. She portions out my one-tenth cut. "I knew you'd come around," she says. She smiles at me with her empty gumline.

"Guess again. I didn't come around. This is just a temporary arrangement."

"That's fine, whatever you say" she says. "I need to take the cleaver and knife back now that you're finished." I guess I'm not lucky enough to get a free weapon out of this arrangement. She begins gumming a raw piece of raven. "Are you going to use that?" she asks, motioning toward the ChapStick.

"It's all gone. The tube's empty," I say.

"Okay. I just want to pretend. You know?" she says. I'm not entirely sure what she's talking about, but I give her the ChapStick anyway. She smiles and smears nonexistent lip balm on her lips. She smiles her gummy smile again, and she heads back to the hotel.

I sample little bits of each cut for dinner. The raccoon tastes best. The raven is okay. The rat is the worst. It's like eating bile—the flesh is spindly and seems pre-digested, and it's overly acidic. I cook my portion of Napping-Woman's leg, searing it to a crisp so that I might boil and burn away any potential diseases. It looks more like a piece of charcoal than a piece of meat now. I smell the piece of human flesh. I even lick the charred exterior, but I don't take an actual bite of it. I decide that whatever happens, I'm still not a cannibal. I push the extra meat into the cold mud—my best attempt at refrigeration.

Another storm rolls in at night, worse than the last one. It's a disgusting whirlwind that's equal parts soot and dirt. I take off my panties and tie them over my mouth like a bandana. This makeshift facemask does a surprisingly good job at keeping dust out of my nose and mouth. I breathe through the Hanes-brand fibers, and I'm grateful that I hadn't been wearing some lacey thong last Tuesday—that Victoria's Secret bullshit wouldn't have helped a bit. My fire goes out as the blinding dirt continues. I think about retreating toward the large fire barrel in the center of town, but I decide against it. It seems like a concession that puts me on the path toward becoming a townie. I just got away from the fire barrel; I'm not going back. I make my way into the burnt forest and find a fallen log for shelter. A layer of dirt accumulates on my body, and it helps trap warmth. I reluctantly sleep in my own filth.

Chapter 4

Everything is coated in a brownish film by morning. I still want to be fractionally cleaner than the townies, but this dust storm has complicated things. I try to clean myself in the river with zero success. The river might as well be pure sludge. It's brown and green. I smell the algae blooms to see if maybe the sludge is edible, but it smells like sewage. The only life in this river appears to be spiders and flies. The spiders range between ping pong ball sized to gigantic baseball sized things. They all have black and yellow markings on their fat hind parts. The spiders don't even bother with webs. They move across floating sticks and gorge on piles of sickly flies. The flies hop around but rarely go airborne. I have no idea how the townies planned on using my blouse for fishing in this shitty river.

I jump up and down and try to shake off the nighttime dirt and soot. I take off my clothes and beat them out like rugs. When I get dressed, there is a noticeable difference. I am not clean, but at least I'm less grimy than the others. I check the tally marks on my blouse and add a fourth day. I ask Condom-Eye how often these dirt storms happen. He shrugs. There doesn't seem to be much this dumbass knows or is good at. I don't know why Tarp-Woman blindly credits him with her survival. I think he'd be dead and eaten by now if not for her.

I look at my pile of sticks and know that I need more than a fire to keep me safe at night. I need to forage for shelter-building materials, but I cannot risk missing the next bus—especially now that I have plenty of change jingling in my Folgers tin. I find Naked-Boy, who is no longer naked, and I show him my credit cards. "What do you do with them?" he asks.

"I'll show you," I say. I sit on a boulder. Naked-Boy plops down in the mud as if it were a comfortable chair. I deal out the credit cards and teach him how to play Go Fish. With the limited card varieties, the game doesn't last long. But I think it's the first time he's ever heard of such a game, and Naked-Boy is entranced.

"Do you have any MasterCards?" he asks.

"Go fish!" I say. Then I ask "Do you have any Visa cards?"

Naked-Boy smiles and nods. He is so excited to play that he doesn't even care that he's losing. He pins his cards to his chest with his wrist-nub. He pinches two cards between his thumb and ring finger and tosses them over. I'm impressed at how easily he uses his remaining hand and fingers—it's almost like he isn't missing the appendages at all. I'm also impressed that Tarp-Woman has bothered to teach him how to read. I wonder if she has a book or two hidden in her shanty, or perhaps they've practiced using discarded wrappers and torn newspaper pages.

"Do you have any *Sea-tell* Public *Lib-ree* cards?" he asks, struggling through *Seattle* and *Library*.

"That shouldn't be in the deck. There aren't any matches for that one," I say. I take the card and tell him he can have a redo.

After we play three games of Go Fish, I hold up the cards

and say "You can have all these cards if you do me a favor. Okay?"

"Sure, anything!" he says.

"I'm going into the forest. I want you to sit right here and watch for the bus. If the bus comes, you need to start shouting as loud as you can. Keep shouting until I come back. I need you to do this for me all day. Then you get to keep the cards. Got it?"

He nods. I hold out the cards and he snatches them between his two fingers. He fans out the deck of credit cards and asks "Can we play one more game first?"

"No, I need to get going. Maybe some other time, okay?"

The hill's bounty is covered in grime from the dirt storm. I brush off items one-by-one, like unwrapping presents that nobody wants. I unearth charred Barbie dolls, an empty roll of tape, a child-sized retainer, a Twix wrapper, and other junk. Useful items include a soggy stuffed animal, four dry cleaner hangers, a weathered pair of Air Jordan sneakers, and a few pieces of cardboard. I carry these items back to my dirt patch on the outskirts of Out of Service. Naked-Boy is still watching for the bus. He asks about Go Fish again, and I remind him that I'm busy all day.

I assemble a shelter using the salvaged forest items. I make sure that my shanty is far enough from Out of Service that the townies will leave me alone. I gut the stuffed animal and tear its hide into strips. I plant ashen sticks in the mud and tie them together with what's left of the Air Jordan laces and pieces of the stuffed animal. I untwist the hangers and use the bendable metal for some additional support. I drape the cardboard over the rickety framework and try my best to keep it in-place with rocks and some mud slathered over the seams. I hope that the sheer weight of the muddy exterior will keep it from blowing off in the next storm. My shanty is definitely shittier than anybody else's; I remind myself that it's temporary.

I head back into the hills looking for more trinkets. I chew on a piece of raccoon flesh and explore the hills as far as possible before running into what Tarp-Woman says are Cleveland Faction totems, each adorned with dangling body parts. There are no heads, but the limbs and torsos all have messages carved onto the overly-scarred flesh. I decide I have an answer for Scarred-Back's back—it must be a latent custom of the Cleveland Faction, adopted long before they were driven into the hills. Most of the totems say things like *Trespassers Will Be Eaten On Sight.* One just says *Fuck Off.* I appreciate the simplicity of that sign. It's not worth the risk to test the enforcement of these warnings. I'm not dying today. Maybe if the bus doesn't come in another few days—and maybe after I've found a good weapon—then I can venture deeper into the forest and the hills, testing the base of the mountain, searching for another escape. The tree branches are all so brittle that they'd disintegrate when used as a bludgeon. Rocks are big enough to kill rats, but too small to harm humans. It's like this entire natural environment is set-up to be as harsh and unforgiving as possible while simultaneously making itself unusable as a mode of defense. For now, I'll keep waiting for the bus and preparing my shanty for the next dirt storm.

I hope I can eventually find something like a blanket or Tarp-Woman's tarp, and I keep an eye peeled for any toys that I can use to bribe Naked-Boy again. I find a one-foot section of a ratty old quilt and a deflated basketball.

Chapter 5

I get up at dawn. At least I think it's dawn. There's still no overt light, but there's a faint fog of something glowing on the horizon, which I interpret as sunrise. Either way, it's early. I want to leave before Chicago Prophet tries to get me into the hotel for a sermon—I know I need to listen to his bullshit soon, but I'm trying to avoid it as long as possible. It's been three days since I butchered his meats, and I still haven't visited the hotel. The bus has not returned yet. My shanty is becoming sturdier, with Tupperware lids, pieces of a tattered rain poncho, and clothespins adding new layers of support.

I place Naked-Boy on bus-watch duty again. Just like yesterday and the day before. He is wearing the gutted Air Jordans. He throws his deflated basketball, trying to make it land inside an arbitrary ring that I've drawn in the dirt. It flops down outside the ring. He scoops up the ball with his fingers and wrist-nub. "You'll get better. Keep practicing," I call out. He lost interest in Go Fish after the first day—you can only play with a limited deck so many times before it gets old. I also must admit that yesterday's broken wristwatch was never much fun—I tried to tell him that it was a futuristic communication device or a spy watch, but he had no frame of reference and just ended up tossing it around. Still, the basketball situation continues to hold his interest.

By midday, my latest haul includes a discarded candle, a cracked yo-yo, and a dirty Virginia Slims pack with one cigarette left. I smoke half of it and save the rest. The candle will be overtly useful, and the yo-yo string may come in handy for hemming together bits of my shelter during the next dirt storm.

A man with no legs crawls out from the totem line. I've never seen him before. He must be from the Cleveland Faction. He picks up the brick that was taken to the hills days earlier, when Napping-Woman's corpse was dumped off the bus. He sets down a cracked picture frame in its place. The frame still holds a stock photo of a married couple. This borderland area must be some kind of trading post for Out of Service and the Cleveland Faction, and I have been stealing from it.

Naked-Boy performs his simple job perfectly. He shouts at the top of his lungs. I run back to town as fast as I can. A bus with *Out of Service* on the marquee idles. "Hold the doors!" I call out to the driver. I do not recognize this driver.

Thankfully this bus is picking up. I dump exact change into that bucket-like thing by the door that gobbles up fares. Even though there is a different person behind the wheel, I think it's the same bus—there's a red stain near the door in the exact spot where Napping-Woman had been dangling. I smile at Other-Driver. He smiles back. Maybe he's glad to actually have a passenger. He adjusts his beaded seat cover; there's a holstered revolver on his belt. I find my seat, fold my hands in my lap, and look out the window at nothingness as we pass through the dark tunnel. This is it. I can finally see where this bus actually goes. I'm sure Tarp-Woman is telling the truth—I know I will be dropped off at my starting point—but maybe I can spot something in the darkness, some vestige of a different destination that I can use to my advantage. And if there's any sign of actual civilization inside the tunnel, I will do whatever is necessary to leave. I'll shatter a window and jump out while the bus is moving if I have to.

The bus lights flicker. It makes a few turns, and I have no idea how Other-Driver knows where he's going. I toe the yellow line near the front of the bus and try to see road, dirt, fog, anything. There is just blackness. It's like the bus is floating in space. I lean forward and my toe slips. "Do not step over the line!" Other-Driver barks. His hand is already hovering near that gun, waiting to draw like some Wild West gunslinger.

"Sorry," I say. I scoot back. I keep track of the exact number and frequency of turns because that is all I have to go off of. There are more left turns than right turns. I want to ask the driver how long he's been on this route. Does he know it by feel rather than sight? Before I say anything, he preemptively taps the *Please Do Not Disturb Driver* sign. I take my seat. I don't want to learn whether or not he's got the expert aim that his cowboy deadeye persona suggests. I'm not dying today. The bus continues for a couple hours. There is no change in the black surroundings.

When the bus finally emerges from the tunnel, I see *Welcome to Out of Service* again. Other-Driver opens the accordion doors

51

and says "Have a nice day!" in his cheeriest inflection. His hand twitches by the holster, waiting for a response.

"Thanks. Hope you have a nice day too!" I say, stepping down from the bus as if it's my normal stop and he's my normal bus driver.

The townspeople converge on the bus. I tell them "You're wasting your time. Don't you recognize me? I'm not a newcomer. You already took my stuff." I spread out my arms, displaying the mud all over my limbs and the scars on my wrists, thinking that dirt and injury are convincing signals that I've been here before.

"We know. Chicago-Prophet wants to see you," says a balding thug with a shattered piece of a guitar neck—the guitar chunk isn't very long, but it's been whittled to a deadly point.

"You're overdue for a visit," Ass-Starer chimes in—that little shit.

"Okay, let's get this over with," I say. I'm already in a shitty mood now that the bus has proved useless, so piling on more misery won't make much difference.

Chicago-Prophet dismisses his guards but keeps his big-ass shotgun handy. He glares at me for a while. "Do you want to renegotiate the contract?" he finally asks.

"No," I say. "I've butchered once batch of meat, and I'm here for one sermon."

"True," he says. "I just thought you'd visit sooner."

"I'm here now," I say. "I'm having a bad day. Let's get this over with."

"I was told that you finally got onto the bus. I thought this would be a good day for you," he says.

"Every day here is a bad day," I explain. "I'm not here to chitchat. I'm here for your sermon."

"Fair enough." Chicago-Prophet retrieves some scraps of paper, napkins, and McDonald's wrappers from a binder. The binder is caked in mud, but I think it's got *Dora the Explorer* on the cover, and that doughnut insignia is etched into it. Chicago-Prophet takes off his thick coonskin cloak and puts on a pair of reading glasses. As far as I can tell, the glasses have no lenses. He flattens the crinkly papers and clears his throat. He starts reading from these pages. He tells me all about Chicago and how there will be a place called Old Country Buffet that has endless troughs of food. And there will be barbeques in a well-manicured city park where the faithful will enjoy beer and bratwurst and ribs. There's also a shitload of information about some wild orgies that will happen shortly after arrival. As he keeps explaining the prophecies, I get the impression that Chicago is their initial reward, but the airport will offer something like heaven or afterlife. The diehard followers only get to fly to the Bahamas after they've proven themselves worthy in Chicago. Exactly how followers prove their worth is unclear.

He goes on to list a bunch of rules and decrees that all followers must adhere too. There are lots of gray areas and cannibalism is semi-encouraged—but only after somebody has already died from other causes. Beneath the gray tones, there are hard-and-fast rules about helping Chicago Faction followers, and how each person has a specific job that helps the collective. Overall, it does sound like this cult has a rudimentary sense of community. There's also a skeletal moral code. It's pretty basic, but I'm glad to hear that there are some harsh torture-like penalties for sexual assault. And murder is only okay in certain instances—most of which involve internal squabbles more than external ones. So at least there's a level of order here, and despite the menacing shitheads roaming around this place, I feel semi-certain that I won't get my throat slit in my sleep. I'm still not sold on the whole concept of this bullshit, but it seems like Chicago-Prophet runs a tight, orderly, authoritarian regime. I get the sense that I'd probably be banished to the hills if I didn't provide much-needed butchery services for him and his followers. For now, our arrangement works.

After a series of verbose descriptions full of "thee" and "thou" and "so sayeth," he tells me that he learned all about the miracle bus and moral code on a pilgrimage into the burnt forest. In any other situation—like one without a shotgun—I might tell this jackass that his scriptures are too rambly. He's jumping all over the place. He should've started with the pilgrimage so the listener had more context for his visions of the Chicago promised land. He tells me all about his journey—which really sounds more like a two-hour hike than a journey—and he explains that the clouds parted and there was a bright light. If this part of the story is true, I can see how he might confuse it for divine intervention since it's always overcast here—pure, unadulterated sunlight is a borderline miracle. He says the sunbeam illuminated a sacred artifact from a Chicago baseball team, and a voice spoke to him and dictated these sacred texts, and he began writing them all down when he returned to Out of Service.

He closes the binder and says "That's all for now. Next time, we'll start on Chapter Two." He pats a stack of cardboard with writing scrawled on it.

"Wait, so what was the sign? Was it the Cubs or the Sox?" I ask, considering the two competing shrines that the Chicago Faction followers worship.

"Well, that's a matter of faith," he says. This bullshit answer is unsatisfying, but he calls for the guards before I can pry further. The guy with the makeshift spear ushers me out.

Newspaper-Guy's corpse is waiting outside my shanty. At least I think it's him. I'm not positive because I can't recognize him without his newspaper, and ravens have eaten out the eyeballs. He really could be any of the townspeople, or he could be nobody. Ass-Starer has a more distinctive, roundish face and a telltale propensity for asses; if he dies, I'll know for sure. I'd almost be glad to see the little shit go.

The body is badly decomposed. I have not seen Newspaper-Guy since the first day. Maybe he's been dead this whole time. I walk back over to the hotel. Chicago-Prophet comes out to greet me.

"I don't want to do humans," I say.

"You did that other woman's leg," he argues.

"Yeah, I know. But I'm not doing it again. Okay?" I say.

"Okay," he says, holding up his hands as if I've offended him. "We'll probably have some more rats soon. There was a swarm of them near the river this morning. I've got some guys tracking them down."

"Do rats really swarm?"

"Around here there do," he says, retreating to his rusted bus and its toilet throne.

Ass-Starer and another crony drag away Newspaper-Guy's body. They hack at it with the cleaver. His head comes off and sinks in the mud. They pull it out and rip out the tongue. They take it to the hotel. I guess tongue is a delicacy.

Chapter 6

I keep testing the bus line to see if there is any hope, but the destination always reads *Out of Service*, and sure enough it always drops me back in town. Aside from making me a local curiosity, the bus trips don't accomplish much. There is no consistency to the number or direction of turns, and the trip's duration varies each time. There are no stops, not even brief pauses. There must be other tunnels diverging from the main tunnel, and the drivers use these labyrinths to keep me guessing. I track it all on a Taco Bell wrapper that I find in the burnt forest. I cannot decipher a pattern. Maybe there is no pattern.

Bus-Driver, Other-Driver, and Another-Driver all direct me to the *Please Do Not Disturb Driver* sign and show me their guns whenever I try to ask questions. So I think of all the questions I want to ask, and I jot the entire list on a DiGiorno frozen pizza box: *Will a bus to Chicago ever come? Will a bus to Pittsburg ever come? Will a bus to Cleveland ever come? Why does the tunnel lead nowhere? Why do you bring newcomers here? Why did you bring me here? Can I please leave? Why do you shoot at us if we don't follow the bus rules? Are you scared of us? How long has this place existed? Will you ever stop coming here? Is this place hell? Do I deserve to be here?* I rip the questions off, splitting the list into individual, pocket-sized bits of cardboard. I covertly slip a couple questions into the driver's pocket each time I exit the bus.

Bus pick-ups happen every couple days—I guess it's not the slow season yet. When I hear the low hiss of the air brakes, I have a few minutes to run, get change from my Folgers tin, and run back. Naked-Boy still alerts me if he happens to notice the bus, but I've run out of potential toys to bribe him with, so his help is not a guarantee. The townspeople watch me scramble for the pick-up buses like it's some reality TV show.

I find it equally amusing how they gather around the drop-off buses. I have little interest in their creepy welcome. I think I'm not technically allowed to participate anyway, since I'm not a member of any faction. Most of the passengers have nothing of value anyway. Occasionally, the passengers aren't even alive. The bullet-riddled corpse dumps remind me why I should not test the patience of these short-fused drivers.

After the townies have scavenged for goods and hassled surviving passengers about factions, I have fleeting conversations with newcomers. Mostly, I ask what city they're from—the drop-off buses come from Portland, New York, New Orleans, Miami, everywhere, and nowhere. I also ask if they can retrace their route through the tunnel. The answer is always "No."

Newcomers become bona fide townies within a day or so. It's ridiculous how quickly people give up and start praising Chicago, eating rat flesh, and sleeping in heaps at the center of town. I continue cutting meat and picking up loose change. This occasional supply of newcomers hasn't replenished my Folgers tin as fast as I'd like.

Today, the bus drops off just one passenger. The townies swarm per usual. I keep my distance and watch for scattered nickels and dimes. The passenger shrieks and pulls out a Taser. In response, she's beaten with various bludgeoning instruments and sliced with a few sharpened objects. Self-defense, I guess. Ass-Starer twists his broken bottle into her stomach. He pulls the bottle in and out several times, blood rising like a geyser. He's got this sick grin the whole goddamn time.

Toothless-Teen just stands there and watches, close enough that she gets splattered with blood droplets, but far enough that she might tell herself she's not complicit. Condom-Eye isn't anywhere to be found. Naked-Boy runs and crouches by Tarp-Woman. She takes the hem of her blue plastic garment and uses it to cover the child's face. When the townspeople have finished smashing the woman's entire body into an unrecognizable paste, they pick up the Taser and test it. The damned thing doesn't even work—the batteries must be dead. I laugh, and I hate myself for it.

I check the tallies on my blouse. It's been sixteen days. I've taken five bus rides so far, and I have zero answers. I must try something else. I must go into the hills. At least until my Folgers tin fills up again. Toothless-Teen licks blood off her arms and meanders over to my shanty. I duck behind a pile of brittle sticks, but she has no trouble finding me. "Time for another sermon," she says.

"I'm not cutting up that woman. I don't do humans," I say.

"You still haven't listened to the prophet's teachings since the last batch. Remember? The ravens?"

"What! That counts? There were just four birds. How does that count?"

Toothless-Teen shrugs. The usual batch of guards approach to intimidate me into complying. Ass-Starer sees the mob forming and is quick to join. He's still covered in the woman's blood, and he's still got that fucking grin. "Fine, I'm coming," I say.

The guards wait outside. Chicago-Prophet already has his lensless glasses on. A Transformers trapper keeper sits in his lap. It's opened to a page that is written on actual paper—soggy, stained paper, but paper nonetheless. "Any thoughts on joining the Chicago Faction yet?" he asks.

"Any thoughts on letting me keep the cleaver?" I ask.

"Why?" he closes the binder.

"For protection," I say.

"The Chicago Faction followers won't hurt you. We've got an arrangement, remember?"

"Sure."

"And the Pittsburg Faction is harmless. There's only three or four of them left."

"What about the hill people?" I ask.

"The Cleveland Faction? They haven't raided Out of Service in a long time. At least a year or so. You're safe here with us," he insists.

I don't tell him that I want to walk into the hills, past the corpse totems. I know he will say it's a bad idea. "I would just feel more comfortable with a weapon," I say.

"You've proven yourself unstable and violent in the past," he reminds me.

I want to scream at him and say that this whole fucking place is unstable. I want to remind him that a woman died moments earlier. I want to tell him that he's a fucking loon, and these twenty-minute sermons are becoming less and less worth the payoff. But he still has that shotgun. "I'm not dying today," I say. This is the first time I've spoken these words out-loud, but it has been my singular rallying cry since the first day.

"Of course not. Why would you think—?" He pauses and holds up the shotgun. "This? It's harmless," he says.

"Not really," I say. Shotguns are one-billion-percent the opposite of harmless.

"I guess we do put up a rather tough front," he says, as if the townies are actually cuddly bunnies without the shotgun and their numerous bludgeoning instruments. I'm pretty sure I'd still be wary of the Chicago Faction diehards regardless of their armaments. "But I don't want to give up the cleaver. How often will something like that get left on a bus again?"

I shrug. I don't know how it was even possible the first time. Half the trinkets in Out of Service have no logical place on a city bus. Chicago-Prophet reaches behind his porcelain throne and pulls out a claw hammer. He presents it to me and smiles. I want to take it and run to the hills now. I want to run into Cleveland Faction territory and kill anything in my path, bounding over the gray mountain in a single leap, into the sunny world beyond. But I need to listen to this dipshit's sermon first, otherwise the guards will detain me.

"So where were we?" he asks, opening back up the Transformers tome. He's smiling, presumably pleased with himself, as if gifting me a little bit of self-defense was his charity work for the day.

"I don't know," I say. He frowns. I promised to sit through his nonsense, but I never promised to listen to it. It's all the same repetitive shit anyway. Over and over, it's just endless talk about how amazing Chicago is going to be.

"I think we were getting into the signs," he says.

"That sounds right," I agree. Like any good prophecy, there are heavenly signs when the prophecy is on the verge of fulfillment.

He tells me about the plagues. He says the land will be overrun with vermin, and rivers will turn to shit, and forests will become ash. His prophetic signs are just a paint-by-numbers description of this shithole place. But he claims that this place was once exactly like Chicago, with rainbows and sunflowers and all-you-can-eat buffets and orgies. Sort of like Out of Service used to be the Garden of Eden or something.

"Uh, huh," I say. "Does anybody else remember this place being lush and green?"

"No. I've been here longer than anybody," Chicago-Prophet says. He looks proud of this fact. I begin to feel something like pity for him. Not pity exactly, but close. Maybe it's more like curiosity mixed with a twinge of empathy. I look him up and down—this aging man with his mud-caked wrinkles, bloody hands, countless scars, black teeth, and beetles crawling around his toilet throne. I wonder if he tried to escape when he first got here. I bet he schemed and plotted. I bet he rode the buses. I bet he actually did go on a pilgrimage into the woods, searching for a way out. I doubt there were any miraculous voices or visions of Chicago, but he probably wandered around looking for escapes, just like me. When he didn't find any, he became this prophet. This cult leader who helps people find a twisted semblance of hope. This shotgun-toting man who would join together a haggard community, trying to make a life here—a shitty, miserable life but a life nonetheless.

"Thanks for the hammer," I say, sensing that we've neared the end of another chapter.

"You're welcome," he says. I wonder why he's so hell-bent on converting me. Maybe after all this time, he's convinced himself that it's all real.

I pass by Naked-Boy on my way out of town. He is rifling through what's left of the dead newcomer's purse. He finds several credit cards to add to his collection. "I thought you didn't like Go Fish anymore," I say.

"I like it. But the games are too short. Now I can play longer!" he says, holding up seven new cards. "I have others too. I've been collecting them."

"How many do you have?"

He thinks for a few seconds. "Forty-one."

"Wow, that's probably enough to play some other games," I say. His eyes widen, as if he's never considered that other card games might exist. "If you let me borrow your sneakers, I'll teach you a new card game tomorrow. Deal?" I'm not sure what I'll teach him—poker seems too complicated for a kid his age, but war might work. He retrieves the Air Jordans, and I pull the laces off my shanty—a section of cardboard wall falls down, but I can always fix that later.

I lace up the sneakers and approach the totems cautiously. I don't know where these hanging bodies are coming from. Maybe these people are townies who wandered too deep into Cleveland Faction territory. Maybe they are Cleveland Faction followers who stepped out of line. There are ten corpses dotting the edge of the territory. They're a strange mixture of part-mummified, part-rotted—like certain pieces began drying out in the dirt storms while other bits remained damp with mud and blood and bile, turning to a foul mush. One of the bodies looks like it's only a day or two old, but I do not recognize the person. Of course, I still don't know all of the townies, so it could be somebody from Out of Service.

Carved into the newest corpse's flesh is yet another message: *Abandon All Hope Ye Motherfuckers.* Not quite Dante, but simply stated and elegant. I try to conceal my newly acquired claw hammer behind my wrist, but it's bulky and awkward. I peer through the forest to make sure I'm not being watched. I cross the totem line. I lower myself into a crouch and begin scuttling up the hills. After a few hundred feet, I realize that these sickly trees leave little to crouch behind, so I stand up straight. I walk slowly. As I move up the hill, the ground becomes less muddy, and broken sticks crunch under my weight.

I stop and listen. The wind is picking up, and I hope I don't get caught in a dirt storm out here—I didn't bring my panty facemask with me. I move another few hundred feet and stop. I move. The trees creak. Another few hundred feet, and this time there is a distinctive crunch, a latent footfall after I've stopped moving. I take two more steps and then abruptly stop. Three crunches come from somewhere to my right. I look but don't see anybody. I ready my claw hammer. I've only been here for ten or fifteen minutes, and I'm already being followed. I thought I'd get at least half-way up the hills before I encountered anybody.

I run. The largest burnt trees are fairly easy to dodge, and the little spindly ones break apart as I push forward. The ground becomes increasingly solid, and I find my footing. The Air Jordans are a bit too small for my feet, but they're lightning compared to my loafers. I sprint through the forest while glancing over my shoulder. I can't tell if I'm being pursued.

The burnt trees give way to living ones. They are sickly looking, and they're still ash-like, but they're healthy enough to retain gray leaves and some blackened bark. I have to turn more deliberately to avoid these obstacles. My pulse pounds in my temples. I take deep breaths. I haven't exactly been hitting the gym lately—my main workout has been an occasional jog to catch the bus, and I'm sure rat carcasses don't provide enough nutrients to sustain this physical activity. My vision briefly blurs and doubles. I have to stop before I pass out, run straight into a tree, or both. I spin around and grip the claw hammer tightly. The broken trees continue to crunch, but I don't see anybody. The crunching stops.

"Why are you here?" a voice calls.

"I just want to see the mountains. I want to see if I can climb them," I say.

"That's what they all want."

"All?" I think about Chicago-Prophet's pilgrimage into the burnt forest and how he heard a disembodied voice. Is that what's happening here? Am I going batshit crazy?

"The others. Those who venture into our territory," the voice explains.

"You're part of the Cleveland Faction?" I ask.

"Yes."

"I'm not with any faction," I say.

"Everybody has a faction," the voice says.

"Not me. I don't mean you any harm," I insist. I decide that if he doesn't believe me, then maybe I'll tell some lie about converting or defecting or some bullshit like that.

"If you're truly factionless, then we don't want to fight with you. But we'll need to administer the test to see if you're sympathetic to the Cleveland Faction. All who wander these woods must take the test," the voice says.

Whatever the fuck the test is, I'm sure it's something twisted. Everything in this place is fucked up. It's not like this mystery voice is going to give me pen, paper, and Scantron for my pop quiz. "Sure, I'll take the test," I say. I glance around to see if there is any place I can run and hide. There's nothing but trees.

Crunching sounds approach, and a man emerges from behind some leaves. He's nude, and he's rubbed soot all over his body, a perfect camouflage for these ashen surroundings.

"I'll take you to camp, and we'll administer the test," Soot-Man says. He's holding an axe in his right hand. His left hand is clenched into a fist. He's got metal washers around each finger, acting a lot like brass knuckles. This might not be a fight that my claw hammer can win. I'm already out of breath from the run.

Before I can fully weigh my options, Soot-Man punches my arm with his washer knuckles. I flinch and release the hammer. He snatches it up. He's got the swiftness and adrenaline of somebody raised on protein powder and meth.

I walk a few paces in front of him, and he tells me where to go. It all looks the same to me, but I think we're still going up a gentle slope, toward the mountains. There's a fire up ahead, and several trees have been knocked over, creating a circular clearing. Some uprooted trees have been sharpened into points, and they form a partial palisade. I gently touch part of

67

the barrier, and it crumbles in my hand—it's all for show; the palisade is brittle and offers little protection. "Keep moving," Soot-Man instructs. I wipe the ash on my slacks and keep walking, toward the fire. If this hillside camp is anything like Out of Service, the fire must be the center.

Two people emerge from a nearby hut made of Wal-Mart bags, mud, and a tattered kite. One is a bald woman, also nude, covered in ash. She's got a dirty gold necklace around her neck—or it might be a locket containing some picture from her former life. She's palming a box-cutter. The other person is a man. He is relatively well-clothed by shantytown standards; he's got some half-disintegrated T-shirt from the 2008 Summer Olympics in Beijing, and he's fashioned a kilt from some carpet samples. He's carrying a baseball bat. Soot-Man whispers to Olympic-Man. Necklace-Woman leans in and adds something to their muted conversation. All three of them look at me. They smile. I don't mind it when Naked-Boy smiles, but everybody else in this place looks sinister when they smile. It's fucked up.

Soot-Man retreats into a nearby hut. When he returns, he's wearing a Cleveland Indians jersey, and he's holding a jumbo Tupperware container—I wonder if my shanty's Tupperware lids all came from the same eight- or twelve- or twenty-piece set as this container. Inside the container are several spiders. They have the same black-and-yellow markings as the spiders from the septic river. Soot-Man opens the lid. I expect the spiders to crawl out, but they just keep wiggling on the bottom of the container. Soot-Man pulls out a large spider and says "Like this. This is how you do it." He demonstrates whatever the hell he's talking about. He holds the spider between his teeth and then bites off the spider's fat hind parts.

"You need the back half. The front half does no good. And there's always a chance it'll bite you if you start with the front," Necklace-Woman tells me. Soot-Man swallows and closes his eyes. He makes a noise that's equal parts relieved sigh and creepy pervert groan.

Necklace-Woman takes a spider and places it in her teeth. The golf-ball-sized thing tries to squirm forward, but she holds her palm flat against her lips, preventing it from wriggling free. She bites down, spits out the spider's front half, and swallows the back half. "Your turn," she says, holding up the Tupperware. There are four spiders left.

"What about him? There are plenty to go around," I say, pointing to Olympic-Man.

"It's my job to make sure you eat yours," he says. He holds his baseball bat closer so that I can see the blood speckled across its surface. Soot-Man twists my claw hammer and taps his axe against his naked thigh. Necklace-Woman raises and lowers the blade on her box-cutter.

I hover over the spiders, inspecting them to see which one is the smallest and least disgusting. I'm not dying today, but I also don't like the idea of shoving a spider in my mouth. I've eaten beetles, but a spider seems different—more revolting. Maybe

69

it's the extra legs. "Why am I eating a spider?" I ask. I don't want them to think I'm not complying—especially with all the weapons actively being brandished—so I pick up a spider immediately after asking.

"This is the test!" Soot-Man exclaims. There's a note of joy in his voice.

"So I eat a spider. Then you know I'm not your enemy, and you won't murder me? Right? Just to be clear. All I need to do is eat a spider and we're done," I say. I open my mouth and maneuver the spider into position. I cringe. I squint so that I don't have to see exactly what I'm doing.

"Yes. Eat the spider, then tell us about your vision of Cleveland," Olympic-Man says.

"And you need to do it right, otherwise it doesn't count," Necklace-Woman reminds me. "Remember, eat the back part. Toss the front." She plucks a second spider from the Tupperware. She demonstrates the procedure yet again. This time, she puts the spider between her teeth and does the entire bite-in-half maneuver in a split second.

I can do this. If this is what it takes to get out of this fucked up camp, then I'll bite the spider and be on my way toward those mountains. I press my incisors onto the hardened back part of the spider. The spider's hind legs vibrate inside my mouth, tickling my palate and sliding across my gums. Its front legs wisp over my lips. It's almost soothing in a fucked up way. I bring my teeth together and feel a bit of cold liquid on my tongue. I swallow as fast as possible and flick the front piece away with my fingers.

"There, I did it," I yell. I spit until my mouth is completely dry. The spider tastes like nothing, but I still keep spitting as if purging some invisible arachnid remnant, excising the spider-eating experience from body and memory. "I believe in Cleveland. It's amazing. It's the promised land," I say in my most convincing inflection, like I'm serious and also happy. I remember using the same tone when lying to my asshole husband.

"No, it doesn't work that way," Olympic-Man says. "Besides, there's no way it kicked in yet. Give it another minute."

"What?" I ask.

Soot-Man collapses with a thud behind me. I think he lands on a rock. His nose starts to bleed. Necklace-Woman slurs her words slightly and becomes less coherent. "You do good. So good. Like you? Like necklace. Head good," she drops her boxcutter and pats her bald head. Maybe this is my chance. I begin walking toward Necklace-Woman, hoping I can grab her discarded weapon. I won't be able to take on Olympic-Man's baseball bat in a direct fight, but maybe I can outrun him. He doesn't look as athletic as Soot-Man. My feet move like I'm wearing lead-filled shoes. I take deep breaths, and my eyes water. I'm winded again, worse than earlier, like I've run a marathon that sapped every ounce of energy. I fall to my knees.

Olympic-Man kneels near me. "The spiders are venomous,"

he says. "It'll fuck you up. You'll have a vision of Cleveland. Then we'll know you're not a threat."

I fall over completely. I can't feel most of my body. It's like my head is floating. Olympic-Man drops his bat and grabs a spider from the container. He picks it up and bites it. He's grinning as he slumps down. My vision narrows. I close my eyes, but it doesn't go black. It's more like white. A white void, waiting for something to fill it. Cleveland, perhaps. But given the fucked up nature of this place, I suspect it will be something other than the promised land. I open my eyes. Everything changes.

Chapter 7

YOUR HUSBAND IS DRUNK YOUR APARTMENT IS OVERRUN WITH COCKROACHES YOUR HUSBAND SHITS HIS PANTS YOUR SISTER CUTS HERSELF DO NOT TELL MOMMY YOUR SISTER SLITS OPEN THE PIG THERE IS A BLOOD BUCKET YOU CUT RATTAILS YOUR SISTER DUMPS IT IN THE SLOP SINK YOUR HUSBAND TELLS YOU TO CLEAN IT UP THERE IS A PILE OF RATS YOU CHOP THE PIG INTO PIECES THERE IS A HUMAN BABY WITH AN UMBILICAL CORD WRAPPED AROUND HER NECK

THERE IS A CAT YOUR SISTER EATS HER TOENAILS CREDIT CARD BILLS ARE NEVER PAID THE CAT IS STRANGLED YOUR HUSBAND LICKS A HYPODERMIC NEEDLE YOUR SISTER VOMITS DO NOT TELL MOMMY YOUR HUSBAND BURNS THE ULTRASOUND YOUR EARLOBE RIPS OPEN YOU SWALLOW A CIGARETTE YOUR SISTER BURNS HER FAVORITE PANTS DO NOT TELL MOMMY YOU BREAK A WINDOW YOUR SISTER STEPS ON GLASS SHARDS

MOMMY KICKS THE TELEVISION DADDY HAS NO JAWBONE YOUR BRA UNDERWIRE PIERCES YOUR BREAST MOMMY IMMERSES HER LEFT HAND IN BOILING WATER YOU MEASURE YOUR

BRUISES YOUR SISTER SAYS YOU ARE LUCKY YOU CHECK THE RAT TRAPS YOUR SISTER NAMES A PIG COCKROACHES CRAWL ON YOUR TOES DADDY HAS NO MORE BULLETS YOUR HUSBAND DOES NOT EXIST YET DO NOT TELL DADDY YOUR SISTER HIDES IN THE PANTRY DADDY BLEEDS ALL OVER THE GOOD RUG MOMMY TELLS YOU TO CLEAN IT UP

YOUR HUSBAND GIVES YOU A DIAMOND YOU CUT YOURSELF MOMMY APOLOGIZES YOU FALL ASLEEP ON A PILE A RATS

Chapter 8

I wake up, and Soot-Man's face is in front of mine. His bloody nose has congealed and dried into a blackish smear. He's still passed out. I'm not sure how long it's been. I may have slept for minutes, hours, or even a whole day. I instinctively check the underside of my blouse to count the tally marks. I know the tallies will remain unchanged, but I've come to rely on it as my calendar, and I half-expect that it will keep time all by itself now. It still reads sixteen days.

I retrieve my claw hammer from Soot-Man's limp grip. Somehow, the axe has vanished, otherwise I would grab it too. I get up. Necklace-Woman and Olympic-Man are out cold. A man with no legs is next to Necklace-Woman. He's carving something into her back with a wine corkscrew. I peer at his work: *No Solicitors*. It's less explicitly threatening than the other totems—almost jokey—but it's been spruced up with a skull-and-crossbones drawing.

"You took a small spider, didn't you?" he says, not looking up from his work.

"Yes."

"Smart. Smaller dose. Wake up quicker. No residual dizziness," he says. "These idiots always overdo it. She overdosed." He jabs the corkscrew into the woman's back and leaves it freestanding. He extends his soot-covered fingers and introduces himself as the Cleveland Faction's prophet.

I grip my claw hammer a little tighter. Just knowing that

he's their prophet puts me on edge. I could dash for the woods anytime now. The legless man will be too slow to catch me. I take a few steps backward.

"Relax," he says. "I'm not going to hurt you. You're one of us now," he says. I remember how Tarp-Woman said the same thing on my first day in Out of Service.

"I'm really not in any faction," I say. I brush off as much soot as possible and consider exit points. The palisade has one main opening, but I could easily break through any part of the brittle barrier if necessary.

"Did you have a vision of Cleveland?" he asks.

"Uh, yeah."

"How was it?"

"It was wonderful," I say. No point in needlessly insulting their prophet. For the time being, I'm on the Cleveland Faction's good side. I'd rather not piss off these spider venom junkies living in the hills. I scan the tree line looking for mountain peaks.

"Don't lie. The visions are always fucked up. The mountains are that way," Cleveland-Prophet says, pointing to my left.

"Thanks."

"I mean, really, the mountains are everywhere. They encircle this whole valley. Walk far enough in any direction and you'll hit a mountain," he says with a laugh. "I wish you luck. But you won't find anything there."

I sidestep Cleveland-Prophet and walk out of camp. Olympic-Man moans in his sleep. He claws at the dirt and makes a gurgling sound.

"He'll be fine," Cleveland-Prophet calls out, as if I give a shit. "He's just having a vision." Cleveland-Prophet laughs and continues making his gruesome totem. I wonder if the others will be angry that I've gone. I wonder if I actually passed their test—their prophet seems to think I'm free to go. I think about Chicago-Prophet and his sermons, and I wonder if his pilgrimage involved spider venom.

I continue into the forest. The gray and black leaves give way to thorny vines. I hook my claw hammer around these vines and pull. Ash trees collapse like dominoes each time I tug down a vine. As I press through the fallen debris, thorns stick into the Air Jordan tread. Thankfully, the thorns aren't long enough to pierce all the way through the sole. When I emerge from the brambles, I've got so many vines pressed into the sneakers that they form an entirely new bottom surface, elevating the shoes atop a solid layer of crushed thorns. It's almost like I'm wearing disco-fabulous platform shoes.

Rocks dot the barren hill, and beyond that several mountains stretch into the clouds. I get closer and look straight up. I cannot see the gray tinged sky anymore. All I see is rock. The mountains lean toward the valley, offering an impassible angle. Even if I were an experienced climber—which I'm not—I'd still need some heavy-duty equipment. At the very least, some sort of grappling hook and a rope—two things which do not exist in Out of Service. The closest facsimiles I have are my claw hammer and shoelaces. The hammer might work, but I won't get much done with a thirty-inch shoelace rope. I touch the side of the mountain. It crumbles on contact. There's a layer of dirt and ash on it, probably blown in from years of dirt storms. For a split second I think that maybe I can tunnel out. I plunge my hammer into the crust. There's solid rock twelve inches beneath the fragile surface. No luck. If I'm going to tunnel out, it'll have to be through the gigantic tunnel that already exists. This mountain range is a giant fucking wall. It offers no escape. I'm not sure if I'm disappointed—I almost expected a dead-end. This place is nothing but endless dead-ends. Everything I touch falls apart.

I lean against the mountain and look into the valley. In the center of the valley, the fire barrel flickers and spews a plume of smoke into the sky. The unforgiving landscape looks smaller now, like this whole shitty area is under a dozen miles in diameter. This is the first time I've stopped to consider the dimensions of this shithole. Without any trees or thorns or venom junkies or big-ass shotguns, I'd guess a person could jog from one side to the other in just a few hours.

I'm not sure how long I've been wandering the hills, but I think it'll be night soon. As much as I hate this place, I'm looking forward to getting back to the illusory safety and security of my muddy cardboard roof. I shudder at this thought. I hate that I have even a slight desire to return to my shanty. I wonder if a bus came during my absence, or if there will be meat waiting for me to butcher, or if Naked-Boy has found any more credit cards, or if Toothless-Teen found a better tube of lip balm.

The clouds look less dark from this angle. As the foggy, barely visible sun dips below the horizon, a single beam of light slips through the darkness, just like in Chicago-Prophet's story. I get up and see if the light is shining on anything specific. I expect to find a Milwaukee Brewers bobble-head or a Detroit Tigers baseball cap or something similar. A new legend and a new prophecy. All I find is a dead raven.

Chapter 9

I take inventory of my belongings to make sure nothing was stolen while I was in the hills. It's all still here. I consider my candle. It's a big candle. It'll probably give me five or six hours of burn-time. It won't get me very far in the tunnel, but it's better than nothing. The ash logs I use in my fire pit burn too quickly, and they're hard to control. But if I wrap some damp fabric near the base, maybe I can get thirty-minutes of burn time per log too. I feel the sides of my shanty for anything that I can use. I begin disassembling my shelter bit-by-bit. I tie pieces of the torn-up stuffed animal and quilt scraps onto any sticks that seem solid enough to burn. I still have doubts about my ability to create lasting light, but I need to try. The bus isn't getting me anywhere. I must brave the dark of the tunnel.

There's something cathartic about disassembling my shanty. It's like I'm exorcising any accidental attachment that I have to my shitty hovel. I'm breaking down my living quarters in favor of an escape. It's almost poetic. *Find Hope Ye Motherfuckers*. While I work, my exposed shanty flaps in the dirty wind.

I hear the low hiss of the bus's air brakes. I look through my partially deconstructed wall and see two passengers getting off: a woman and a man. The woman must've been on her way to work. She's got a nice suit and a briefcase. I think the man was a tourist in whatever city they came from. He's holding a map, and he's got a fanny pack. The townspeople gather around and frighten the shit out of them as usual. Toothless-Teen smashes open the woman's suitcase with the butcher's cleaver. Ass-Starer is staring at her like the lecherous little shit that he is. The man scrambles away and runs in my direction. Condom-Eye and another townie chase him. He trips and falls to the ground. Condom-Eye says "We aren't going to hurt you." The other townie spits pus from inside her cheek pocket. They both need to work on their bedside manner.

They take off the man's fanny pack. They dump the contents on the ground. I can't tell what some of the items are, but one object stands out like a glowing beacon: a bottle of Purell. I run over as fast as I can. I grip my claw hammer, willing to fight for it if necessary. "Get off of him!" I scream.

Condom-Eye and the other townie look at me. They each recoil a little at the sight of me running forward. Ass-Starer comes over and asks "What's going on here?"

"This doesn't concern you," I say, pointing at him with the hammer.

"You aren't a member of the Chicago Faction. You can't take part in the welcoming party."

"Welcoming?" Purell-Guy says, gathering his fanny pack contents. "This is a welcome?"

"I want that Purell," I say.

Purell-Guy holds out the bottle. "Take it," he says. There is no fear in his voice, even as I stand there with a claw hammer raised high. Maybe he can sense that I'm desperate. Maybe he's just a good person—if so, that'll get beaten out of him soon enough. "Seriously, take it," he repeats. "It's yours." I want to kiss him. If he can somehow conjure clean water, soap, and shampoo, I'll fuck his brains out.

"It doesn't work that way. You can't just give it to her," Ass-Starer says. "We can use that as an accelerant."

Chicago-Prophet emerges from the hotel to see what all the commotion is about. He's got that shotgun, so we're all on our best behavior. Ass-Starer gives him an inaccurate summary, making it sound like I just took a shit on Chicago Faction tradition. I politely say that I would be willing to barter for the Purell. I throw in a "please" and "thank you" for good measure. Purell-Guy has no idea what the fuck is going on. He checks his map, as if perhaps this is a stop on his touristy route around Baltimore.

"I'll butcher the next batch for half my normal rate," I say. At the mention of butchery, Purell-Guy squirms a little.

"No, you'll do it for free," Chicago-Prophet counters.

"Deal," I say. Really, I'd have agreed to just about any terms. Ten free batches. Twenty. I'd even start carving humans again if necessary. Chicago-Prophet takes the Purell bottle from Purell-Guy and personally walks it over to my shanty. Ass-Starer goes back to harassing the businesswoman while Condom-Eye renews rifling through the rest of the fanny pack. He finds sunglasses, ballpoint pens, house-keys, two granola bars, a small box of raisins, and several crumpled receipts. Purell-Guy crawls away from the scene.

Chicago-Prophet comes back from my shanty holding one of my makeshift torches. "What the hell is this?" he asks, tossing down the torch and stepping on it. The frail wood breaks apart.

"A torch. So what?"

"Why do you need a torch?"

"I'm going into the tunnel," I say.

"What are you trying to pull? First you go on a pilgrimage into the hills, now you're—"

"It wasn't a pilgrimage. I was checking out the mountains."

"Why?"

"I'm trying to get the fuck out of here! I've made that pretty clear since day-one."

"You can't go into the tunnel."

"I'm not a member of the Chicago Faction. You can't give me orders," I remind him. I consider a lengthier rant about his batshit religion, but I refrain. He's still got that big-ass shotgun. He needs my services as a butcher, but I don't want to push the limits of that arrangement.

"You'll get lost in there. You'll starve to death," he says.

"I'll take my chances."

"The rat hunters will be back soon. You'd just better do your damned job before you go," he says. Chicago-Prophet goes back to the hotel, and I hear him smash something inside.

I take off my clothes and rub Purell all over. My skin tingles at the alcohol's slight burn. The hand sanitizer mixes with the dirt and soot, and it forms a viscous paste. The paste begins hardening, but I'm able to scrape some of it off. I do not get myself completely clean, but I've managed to undo several layers of filth. I squirt some Purell into my greasy hair and run my fingers through it. I dab a little Purell on the most disgusting parts of my blouse and pants—large blood stains that have turned brown and blackish. I make sure to leave my tally marks in-tact, and I add a seventeenth day since I didn't get a chance earlier. I also use my eyeliner to mark the outside of my Purell bottle, placing a line across its current level—about half full. I need to keep track of my usage and ration accordingly. And if I ever discover that somebody has used even one drop of my Purell, I will find them and kill them.

I make a few more torches while various hunters drop rats one-by-one into a pile. Tarp-Woman and Condom-Eye drop rat carcasses as a couple. Condom-Eye sees my torches and says "Make sure you get back out before those burn out." I do not thank him for this unsolicited and completely obvious advice.

"I have something for you, honey," Tarp-Woman says. She holds out three tampons. The Kotex warppers are shiny and new.

"No thanks," I say. I appreciate the gesture, but I do not get periods anymore. I don't tell this to Tarp-Woman because I'd rather keep the reason buried. "You keep them." I doubt the townies get periods either—everybody is so malnourished, and I've heard that starving people don't menstruate.

"I don't need them. We're pregnant," she says. She smiles.

85

Condom-Eye pats her still-flat belly.

"Congrats," I say. I turn to my work, chopping off rat heads with the cleaver and delicately slicing meat from tiny bones with the paring knife.

"Well, I just wanted you to know," she says. "I haven't told anybody else yet."

I feel somewhat guilty for the half-hearted reply. I give her my best fake smile. I think she sees through it. Thankfully, she doesn't ask what's wrong.

I continue to chop heads. I pull out tiny rodent entrails. One of the hunters drops a racoon. Its intestines remind me of an umbilical cord. The shithead tries to make small-talk. He's using some ragged fabric like a bandana. He looks like my husband. He looks like the doctor who performed the first surgery and the second and the third—when everything that could go wrong did. He looks like my dad. I wonder what that bandana is hiding. He looks like my sister's favorite pig. I kick his shin. He yelps and curses and hobbles away—maybe he's going to tattle on me, running off to Chicago-Prophet.

I think about the spider venom and wonder if it's possible to take a half-dose. Just a little bit. Something to take the edge off. Something to help me cope without a full-fledged hallucination shouting in my goddamn face.

Purell-Guy wanders over. His clothes are already looking muddy, and I bet he already regrets giving up the hand sanitizer without a fight. I slide the bottle toward the back of my shanty, just in case he has his eye on it. "What?" I ask. I just want to be left alone.

"I wanted to say thanks for saving me," he says.

"I didn't save you. I saved the Purell bottle," I explain.

"I heard you say that you're going into the tunnel."

"Yeah, I am. And I've got work to do. So go away."

"Can I come with you?"

I look up from the pile of rats. Purell-Guy's knuckles are split open and his fists are smeared with blood. I don't think all of the blood is his. Maybe I've underestimated him. "Why?"

"Because I want out."

"They all want out at first," I say. "You'll join the Chicago Faction in a day or two."

He doesn't argue. "Well, maybe that's true. But for now, I want out. There is safety in numbers."

I think it over. I want to tell him to fuck off. But he's not exactly a townie yet, and maybe I'm still grateful for his immediate offer to give up the Purell. I could use another body. He could go in front, like a decoy. He could call out if I lose my way. And he's still eager enough to escape that he'll do any of it. Anything I ask, he will comply. "Okay," I say. "But I need to butcher these rats first. We'll leave tomorrow. You need to make your own torches. You can find sticks and other supplies in the hills. Just don't cross the totems."

"Totems?"

"Just don't. They'll make you eat spiders."

"What? Spiders? I don't—"

I almost find it funny that he's so clueless. I wonder if Tarp-Woman thought I was funny on my first day. I consider my shanty on the edge of town with its pile of rats outside, and I know I must look like a crazed hermit. Purell-Guy must be presuming all sorts of things about me. Maybe he's wondering how long I've been here—seventeen days. Everything turns to shit so fast here. "You can go now," I say. He stands there a moment longer. I grab my hammer and shriek like a banshee. He scurries off to do his assigned task in the burnt forest.

Chapter 10

The candle only illuminates a couple feet in front of us. It smells of lavender and is colored purple. The melted wax forms a warm seal around my left fist. I keep the claw hammer ready in my right hand. The townies let Purell-Guy keep his fanny pack, and it's loaded with rat bones. I ask for a bone every fifty paces; I dip the bones into the purple wax and drop them. These markers serve as our breadcrumbs, leading the way back to town. "Why do you dip them in wax?" he whispers, as if some ghostly tunnel creature might be eavesdropping.

"Because there are already bones on the ground," I say, waving the candle across the tunnel floor, revealing a few scattered bird beaks, rat skulls, and human ribcages. "We need to be able to tell which ones are ours."

The tunnel isn't very wide, and it seems to go in one straight direction, but we still manage to get turned around in the dark. Every twenty or thirty minutes, I check the ground and see a wax-coated bone on the floor. We change tactics and stick close to the tunnel's edge. Purell-Guy goes in front and keeps his hand on the wall. He takes uncertain steps forward while I keep him in-sight with the flickering candle. In my other hand, I have the hammer raised at all times, but I know I won't be able to help if anything happens to him. It's too dark. I'll just swing blindly and run back the way we came. I'll leave him in an instant if I need to.

Purell-Guy begins small-talk bullshit. At first I don't answer.

He keeps asking me questions like it's a coping mechanism. I find the questions less and less annoying as time and darkness drag onward. He phrases his questions in the present-tense. I appreciate this fact—it's like he's certain that a world still exists beyond this tunnel, and he's hopeful that we'll soon find it. I can't help but get sucked into the momentary optimism. "Where are you from?" he asks.

"Seattle," I say.

"Oh, so you can talk! I wasn't sure," he says.

"Don't be a jackass," I say.

"Sorry. Where do you work?"

"A deli."

"Have you ever killed anybody?" he asks.

"What the hell kind of question is that?"

"I don't know. It's just this place, you know? It's like—"

"Yeah, I get it. This place is fucked up," I say, but I still don't answer his question. I want to tell him, but I don't. He moves on to other questions—favorite movies, books, places I have traveled. I tell him what I can remember—it seems so distant now, even though I've only been gone eighteen days. Eventually, he stops asking questions, and I almost miss it. I consider asking him some questions, but I know I shouldn't. It's only a matter of time before Named-Pig is slaughtered and eaten, just like when I was a kid. In the silence, our feet shuffle along the gravely road. I hear something dripping in the distance.

The candle burns out. With no waxy lavender scent, all

we get are overwhelming whiffs of mildew. I light a torch. Purell-Guy wants to light one of his torches too, but I say that it's a waste. One is enough for both of us. "Then why did you have me make my own torches if we're going to share?" he asks.

"Because now we have twice as many," I say. It's a good thing we've got the extras too, because the torches burn out faster than anticipated—a major drawback of using pre-burnt wood from the ash forest. The best torches give us about ten minutes of light. Others last just one or two minutes. We've got a whole bundle of torches—nineteen total—but I don't think it's enough. I consider the candle's burn-time. We've been walking at least five hours. Even if we turn around now, the torches will still burn out before we reach muted shantytown daylight. We either keep going forward, or we sprint back the direction we came. I don't bother to ask Purell-Guy's vote. We push forward and keep to the wall.

We're down to just three torches when I lose sight of Purell-Guy. I don't know how it happens. I'm holding the torch and ready with the hammer. His back is a few inches away, then suddenly everything is black. I take a few quick paces forward. Nothing. I call out, and he does not answer.

I hook the claw hammer on my belt loop and touch the wall. I point the torch forward and keep moving. It burns out in a few minutes. The second burns out even sooner. The third disintegrates before I can light it. "Fuck!" I scream. I get the hammer ready. I keep groping in the dark, moving in what I think is the right direction. My hands slide across rough concrete walls, rubbing my palms raw. There are occasional splotches of mold and slimy things on the tunnel walls, and this cooling sensation soothes the burn. I cannot let go of the wall even for a moment. If I do, I fear that it will disappear.

In another few minutes, the scrape and the slime stop. I'm touching something else. This isn't a wall. It's mostly firm but has modest elasticity. It's warm. I push on the object; there's a shriek, and the thing moves. I bring my claw hammer down onto the shrieking creature. The thing collapses and takes the hammer with it, still embedded in the flesh. I feel the corpse. There is a fanny pack full of bones. I run my hands over Purell-Guy's body and find the hammer lodged in his skull. The hammer is really stuck. I have to pull with both hands and push the head away with my foot to yank it out. There's a loud crack.

I reach out for the wall, and it's gone. I take another few steps. Still nothing. I go back the other way. Nothing again. I pick a direction and keep going. I walk heel-to-toe like a DUI test, making sure I move in a straight line. Eventually, I will run into something. Anything. I trip over another corpse. This one smells and is mushier, like it's been dead for much longer. I get up and keep moving. Eventually the tunnel will lead someplace. I'm not dying today. I shout in the emptiness: "I'm not dying today. You hear me? I'm not fucking dying!"

In something like an hour, I see a fog that half-resembles light. It's muted and gray. I walk out of the black-hole-esque tunnel and back into Out of Service. The townspeople crowd around. They gasp and whisper to themselves. Tarp-Woman covers Naked-Boy's eyes, as if I've somehow become a grotesque monster in a day's time.

Near the fire barrel, there are four dead bodies. Their mouths are gagged and they're wearing blindfolds made of oily rags. Their arms and legs have been chopped off. There are tourniquets on the missing limbs, like somebody wanted to slow the bleeding—either a shitty attempt at treating the wound, or a sadistic effort to prolong a slow death. The Chicago Faction doughnut insignia is carved into their naked chests. I do not bother to ask about these mutilated bodies, and nobody questions my bloody hammer, still dripping a red trail back to my partially disassembled shanty.

Chapter 11

Scarred-Back emerges from his shanty and hobbles out of town, toward my shanty. I don't think I've ever seen him walk. He's always in his shanty—mostly sleeping, occasionally getting things carved into his skin. He's slow. His legs wobble and spasm as he moves. He's got bedsores covering his chest—or I guess they're technically dirtsores since he doesn't have a bed. "I just heard from somebody that today's story is about you," he says. He's excited. Giddy, even. The headline is simple, *Local Woman Survives Tunnel; Hailed as Hero.* "I'm not a local, and I'm definitely not a hero," I say. I fight against the impulse to smile. I don't need these fucked up townies looking up to me. I don't want them to like me. I fucking hate them. I'm getting out of here. I'm getting out. I'm getting out.

Scarred-Back looks confused. "I know you're not a local. What are you talking about?" He probably hasn't heard the story verbatim.

"Never mind," I say. I give Scarred-Back the rest of my Virginia Slims cigarette nub; I think of it like tipping the paper boy. He smells the unlit cigarette for a while before lighting it.

"Is it true?" he asks. "Did you survive the tunnel?"

I guess since he rarely ventures out, he hadn't seen me leave and return.

"Yes."

"What's it like in there?"

"Dark."

He snickers a little. He's got a wheezy laugh.

"You take anybody with you?"

"Yes."

Scarred-Back takes a deep breath. The cigarette burns down to the filter. He inspects the remnant. "And?" he asks.

"He died."

Scarred-Back snickers again. He cuts open the filter and nibbles on its papery, tar-stained innards. "Thanks for the cigarette," he says. I think he tries to wink at me, but his eye doesn't work right. It twitches a little and closes half-way. He limps off.

Naked-Boy comes over at some point, and we play a card game. I show him my latest find: a set of dice. They aren't normal six-sided dice. They're those funky twenty-sided ones designed for more complicated games—I think they're used in *Dungeons & Dragons* and shit like that. Still, they work for a modified version of liar's dice. He goes off to show his mom the new game.

Toothless-Teen walks over next—since when did my shanty become a hotspot? She gives her usual beckoning call: "You're wanted at the hotel." She sounds happier than usual. Her toothless, bloody gums stretch into a smile. She's wearing lipstick and mascara. She must've found the cosmetics in that woman's briefcase—the one who arrived with Purell-Guy. The lipstick is smeared haphazardly across her lips and onto most of her bare gums. I don't think she's ever used makeup before.

"Why are you wearing that?" I ask.

"I wanted to look pretty," she says. "Today is a big day for me."

I think she wants me to press for more information, but I just want to get this hotel visit over with. I have no idea why Chicago-Prophet needs to see me—I'm not due for a sermon—but I know that my refusal will just result in another mob sidling up next to Toothless-Teen. I get up and say "You look nice."

"Thanks," she says, her voice quavers. I can see her blushing even through layers of dirt. "I just wanted to look more like you."

"I don't wear makeup. At least, not anymore," I say.

"I know. That's not what I meant—" she stammers a little and then shakes her head. She picks up the pace to the hotel, nearly breaking into a jog as she goes.

She disappears into the hotel and I follow. She stands beside Chicago-Prophet. He's holding that double-barrel, big-ass sawed-off shotgun. The guards are at attention too.

"So what's up? Sermon?" I ask.

"No. Our arrangement has changed," he says, pointing the gun directly at my chest.

"What do you mean?"

"I hear you're starting a faction," he says.

"Fuck no!" I say.

"Then what about that man who went into the tunnel with you?"

"What about him?"

"He followed you in there. You have followers."

"No I don't! He was just a newcomer who wanted to tag along," I shout.

"People are murmuring. They're starting to talk about new factions. They're starting to question whether or not a bus to Chicago will ever come." I do not respond. I don't want to antagonize him, but I'm also not going to feed into his delusions with some insistence that the Chicago bus is right around the corner. I cross my arms. He continues, louder now, almost yelling: "Those four bodies in the center of town. You know what those are?"

"Yeah, they're dead people," I say.

"They're a message. They are the four remaining Pittsburg Faction followers who refused to denounce their faith. I tried to be reasonable with you. I thought we had a mutual respect in our arrangement. But I've had enough of this bullshit. Law and order is breaking down around here. People are saying crazy things about joining the Butcher Faction."

"There is no Butcher Faction," I insist.

"That's not what I hear. Have you read today's paper? These people look up to you. They admire you."

"Since when? I keep to myself and tell everybody to fuck off. Besides, if there was a Butcher Faction, then why didn't you just round up my followers and kill them? You had to go after the Pittsburg people because I have zero followers. Nada.

Zilch."

"And I'd like to keep it that way," Chicago-Prophet says. "Here's how this is going to work from now on. You're not going into the woods. You're not going into the tunnel. You're not riding the bus. You can walk around town, but that's it. You're going to keep butchering for us. And you're doing humans again. And you're also going to take on an understudy," he says, motioning to Toothless-Teen. She smiles and waves at me like we're being introduced for the first time.

"Why would I do that?"

"Because if you don't, I'll kill you." He waves his hand, dismissing me from his chambers. For now, I think he's bluffing. If he kills me, I'll be a martyr. That'll make his morale problem worse. Then again, once I train Toothless-Teen, he has less incentive to keep me alive. At this point, the pros to killing me outweigh the cons. How the fuck did I make a mortal enemy in just a few weeks' time?

Toothless-Teen grabs the cleaver and paring knife, and she follows me back to my shanty. The four dead Pittsburg Faction followers are piled up outside. I do not recognize any of them. "So what should I do?" Toothless-Teen says, holding up the cleaver.

"Nothing," I say.

"Please! I want to learn," she says. "I've been watching you. I practiced on my own rats."

"Why?"

"Because I want to know how to do things. Nobody has ever showed me how to do things," she says. These are the vaguest terms possible, so I just keep staring until she coughs up a more detailed explanation. "They just send me on errands. I run around and deliver messages. I don't do anything else. I want to learn stuff. I want to be good at something. Like you. You're good at things. You're smart."

"I'm not smart. I'm stubborn. There's a difference," I say. A smart person would give up. A smart person would focus on building a better life here rather than trying to run away.

"But you teach that boy things!" she says. "Why won't you teach me?"

"That's different. I teach him games," I say. "I'm not running a goddamn school. I don't want to be known as the town butcher. All I want is to get out of here. Why does nobody get that? I'm biding time. Any day now, I'll—" I stop mid-sentence because I don't know what else I'm going to do. I don't have a next move. I've ridden the bus. I've wandered the hills and explored the rocky edges of this place. I've braved the tunnel. It seems hopeless. It is hopeless. It's fucked. I don't want to die today, but what else is there to do? What other options do I have but to storm the bus with my insignificant hammer and get blown to bits by the driver's gun?

I reach for the cleaver and Toothless-Teen lets it go. She smiles as if she's about to get her first lesson. I could chop her in half. I could chop off my own arm. I could bleed out like the Pittsburg Faction people. I look at the gray sky and wonder if I've made a tally on my blouse today. I can't even fucking remember. I want to chew another spider and go far, far away from here. I take a deep breath.

"Are you crying?" Toothless-Teen asks.

"No," I scream, but I'm not sure. All I can feel is my blood pumping and my nerves twitching. All I can do is chop up meat, and keep my guard up, and rinse off dirt with my rationed Purell bottle. There is nothing left for me. Nothing but the bus. The bus. There is a second bus. A bus that nobody admits is a bus. "Tell me about the hotel," I say.

"What do you mean?"

"How did it get here?"

"It's just a story. I don't know if it's true," Toothless-Teen says.

"What's the story?"

"The three prophets. Before they were enemies, they killed the driver and took the bus," she says.

"So it can be done," I say.

"Huh?"

"Never mind. Bring me that one, and let's get started," I say, pointing to the smallest corpse. It's a boy about Toothless-Teen's age. In a different life, they might've gone to the same high school. I take off the tourniquets. Partially congealed blood oozes from the wounds. Blackened flesh falls in thick plops. Some sickly flies hop around the wound, unable to get airborne. I go to work. I don't say much, and I make sure to feed Toothless-Teen misinformation. I lead her nimble hands toward the stomach and hope she'll rupture it.

As we work, Toothless-Teen occasionally winces at some unseen pain. I don't see any blood or pus coming from her dirt-smeared body, but it could be any number of hidden ailments—probably a simple case of internal bleeding. Or it could just be the generalized pain of living in this place day-in and day-out. The pain of being a worthless errand girl for psychopathic cultists dreaming of a Chicago bus. The pain of not having a single goddamn thing to look forward to anymore. The pain of escape being impossible. The pain of dirt storms and ash clouds and gnawing on rats and drinking sewage and chopping up dead bodies. Some part of me wants to actually help her. To grab her bony wrist and show her how to cut, how to cleave, how to butcher. How to carve something dead into something that matters. But I can't do it. I cannot take the risk. I will lose all my leverage if I teach this desperate teenager how to steal my job.

By the third body she's learning on her own, despite my attempts at sabotage. She's a natural. She's good at this. I let my hand slip and cut Toothless-Teen's palm. I pretend it's an accident.

She weighs the meat like usual, but she does not leave any. I don't know if this is because my rations have been rescinded by Chicago-Prophet, or if it's because she remembers that I don't eat humans. Either way, she looks sad as she goes. Her mascara is runny and she has licked off most of the smeared lipstick. She wraps a ratty tube sock around the fresh wound on her hand.

Chapter 12

Despite Chicago-Prophet's semi-martial-law, I'm able to wander the town and go about daily survival business. I gather firewood, making sure I don't go too deep into the hills. I repair my shanty after each dirt storm. Despite this minor mobility, I am still unable to go beyond a small perimeter of operation. My claw hammer has been taken away. Chicago-Prophet lets me keep the Purell. Maybe he knows that the hand sanitizer plays a sizable role in my will to live. I keep marking my rationed quantities, but on particularly shitty days, I use two full pumps and wipe off as much dirt as possible. I see my skin. I look at its color and hue and remember that something other than gray and ash and blood exists in the world. I mark my blouse. It's been twenty-six days. Almost a month, and look where I'm at. Worse than when I arrived. Much worse. I wonder how many tally marks it will take for me to fill my blouse. I wonder when the months will turn into years. I wonder if I will even live that long. And if I do survive, when will I settle down with the next man who brings me Purell? When will I start wearing a blue tarp and digging up rocks for my lover?

I try to sneak into the hills, hoping to loot a few more supplies or maybe talk the Cleveland Faction into killing Chicago-Prophet, but Ass-Starer and some other goon are watching me, and they threaten me with decapitation. Ass-Starer sneers at me. He jams the jagged edges of his broken beer bottle into his own palm—I don't know what this is supposed to prove. Maybe he thinks I will be intimidated. He twists the bottle, making a perfect circle, then he gently slices a small circle in the middle. I think it's that stupid doughnut symbol again—even after all the sermons, I have no idea where that iconography comes from. "Uh huh," I say. "I'll head back. Calm the fuck down." I consider what I might do if I still had my claw hammer.

I go to the river and pretend to strain septic water into my burnt soda can. There's a human foot floating in the water. I gather spiders and take them back to my shanty. I peel apart the arachnids while they squirm between my fingers. I squeeze the back parts and harvest individual drops of venom, deposited into an empty can of Bush's Baked Beans. Drop by drop, I begin filling my stash of venom. Soon I will have enough to taint the meat supply. I will splash the accumulated venom over the freshly cut portions. I will add extra venom to any tongues, as these are delicacies reserved for Chicago-Prophet. When they all fall into a drugged-out stupor, I will waltz into the hotel, pick up the shotgun, and overtake the next bus that rolls into town. And if a bus does not come right away, I will sit in the hotel and wait on Chicago-Prophet's throne. I will blast buckshot into anybody who dares to enter. I will wait as long as it takes, and I will never surrender the gun.

Toothless-Teen drops a large plastic tub in front of my shanty. I put away my spider drippings. I kick dirt and mud onto the torn-up spider bits. I think she sees them, but she doesn't say anything—she probably has no idea that these spiders are venomous. Inside the plastic tub, there are three birds. "What the fuck are those?" I ask.

"Ravens," she says.

Technically, I guess she's right. They are ravens. But they're even more sickly than most of the others around here. They're all half bald. One raven's beak points up in the wrong direction. Another has a claw that wraps around backwards. The third has white eyes; I think it's blind because it conks its head into the container a lot. "Okay, so why are you bringing me live ravens?" I ask.

"I thought we could raise them. For eggs or something," she says.

"I don't know how to do that."

"You grew up on a farm, right?"

"We didn't have chickens," I say.

"Oh, well, how hard could it be?"

"Why do you want to raise ravens?"

"I told you. I want to be good at something," she says. She's wearing that smeared lipstick again.

"Your lipstick is smudgy," I say.

She winces that wince of hers, like something has cut her deep. "Can you teach me?" she asks.

"I told you, I don't know about raising birds," I say.

She looks at her toes. "That's not what I meant."

"The lipstick?"

She nods. I consider the possibility that Toothless-Teen was conceived here—just like Naked-Boy; just like Tarp-Woman's unborn child. I wonder if she has ever seen a world outside of this shithole shantytown. I don't know who her parents are—or who they were—they must be dead. To her, I might as well be a supermodel. I have better hygiene than most people here. I still have most of my hair and all my teeth and all my appendages. Even though my breasts are uneven—one barely an A cup, the other a D—Toothless-Teen probably admires the fact that I even have breasts to begin with. The other women here are so malnourished that their chests have shrunk to nothingness. To her, I'm bodily perfection.

She hasn't had the pressure of millions of Photoshopped images raining down on her self-respect, contorting it into some shitty version of self-loathing. She's never skipped a meal because her asshole husband called her fat. Yet somehow, she's picked up whispers of this paradigm—she's heard enough that some part of her knows what lipstick is. And she wants to do it right, to put it on just right, to feel like she looks good just once, to smile without being reminded of her missing teeth and gaunt flesh and fucked up existence in this fucked up place for her entire fucked up life. She's culled this information from the stylized haircuts and pushup bras and stiletto heels of the occasional newcomer. She wants to know what it's like to be pampered. She wants a motherfucking spa day. She'll probably laugh when the spa attendant suggests a mud bath.

I hold out my hand and Toothless-Teen deposits the tube

of lipstick in my palm. She might be better off never knowing anything about makeup, never discovering the shittiness that underlies those *Cosmo* pages occasionally scattered in the hills. But in that moment, I just want to do something nice for her. I want to see her smile again. I wipe off her smeared lipstick and show her how to do it right, more delicately, more precisely, just like slicing meat off the bone.

I want to show her what it looks like in a mirror, but I don't know if a mirror exists in Out of Service, and the septic river is non-reflective, and every piece of metal is rusty in this place. So I describe it to her. I tell her that she reminds me of a famous actress. I tell her that she'd be the goddamn prom queen and king all at once. I tell her that I'm sorry for cutting her hand. I tell her she's good at butchering. I tell her how good she is. Over and over, I tell her that she's good at it. And I tell her that she'll get even better with practice. She's grinning the entire time while I keep telling her all about the different cuts and slices. It's the longest I've spoken to anybody since arriving in Out of Service. We talk about meat. But somehow, I think we're talking about something else too. I think she wants to go with me if I'm ever able to leave, but I'm too scared to ask her.

Chapter 13

The ravens have yet to lay any eggs. I don't know if raven eggs are even edible—although, most of what gets eaten in Out of Service isn't technically all that edible. The entire project seems pointless, but Toothless-Teen is overjoyed with every step of progress.

The ravens try to cannibalize each other. They go for the eyes first. Toothless-Teen finds two additional containers and separates them.

I make a leash from some braided newspaper fibers. I let the ravens out for a few hours every day—they need to get some exercise, I think. They eat flies and venomous spiders. I wonder if the birds hallucinate. One of them spits up some yellowish bile and its beak actually falls off. Another bird pecks at its own leg, snapping it like a twig. They move like they're flightless. When they try to fly, they can only lurch about twenty feet into the air before plummeting down. Even in their dejected and grotesque state, there's something magical about the way the birds move. In their ungraceful and brief ascent, they have escaped—if only for a moment—before plunging to earth.

If my plan to steal the shotgun and overtake the bus fails, perhaps the birds will be useful. If they ever grow strong enough to fly higher and longer, then maybe they can fly away from here, like carrier pigeons. I can attach messages to their stick-thin legs. The ravens will carry my cries for help and pleas for rescue over the mountains, into the sunny world beyond.

I imagine entire flocks of ravens carrying messages to distant castle-like otuposts brimming with rescuers. I guess that makes me the goddamn damsel in distress.

My spider venom reserves fill nearly half the Bush's Baked Beans can, and it's time to use it. Toothless-Teen drags a legless body over to my shanty. I recognize it as Cleveland-Prophet. Toothless-Teen works on the torso while I do the arms and head. I carve out the tongue and drop it directly into the Bush's Baked Beans can.

"What's that for?" Toothless-Teen asks, pointing at the can.

I do not respond. We haven't spoken much since that one time. But I also haven't sliced her hand again, so I think we're on good terms. I gather Toothless-Teen's cuts and shave off some excess gristle. I drip venom on everything until the can runs dry.

She hauls the meat over to the hotel. A few minutes later, she comes back, and I have déjà vu as she repeats her usual errand-girl lines: "You're wanted at the hotel." I haven't been summoned to the hotel since the tunnel and my quarantine. As I walk past the fire barrel, some townies are burning the meat, throwing it directly into the fire. They must know its tainted. I look around for a weapon. There's nothing available, so I scoop up a rock and head into the hotel.

Chicago-Prophet is resting his feet on Condom-Eye's lifeless body. "Along with hunting rats and cleaning the shitter, you know what else this guy does around here?" Chicago-Prophet asks.

I shake my head no, but I have a guess.

"He's my food taster," he says.

"Is he dead?" I ask.

"Why do you care? Isn't this what you wanted?" he asks. "To poison all of us?"

I want to say *No, just you. I wanted the others to pass out,* but I don't. I remind myself that I will get through this. I have to. I must. I cannot die in this fucked up place. I've tried so hard to get out—I've tried everything. I can't just get blown to bits by some guy sitting on a toilet in a rusted-out bus in the middle of fucking nowhere. This isn't how I go. "No. I don't know what you're talking about," I say. I hope that he didn't question Toothless-Teen—she saw me with the spiders and Bush's Baked Beans can on several occasions.

"Really? You didn't want my shotgun? You didn't poison the meat somehow?"

"Have you seen the bodies around here? Do you know how many of them are riddled of maggots and gangrene? I do the best I can, but something like this is bound to happen from time to time."

"I don't buy it. This has spider venom written all over it," Chicago-Prophet says.

"No shit. That guy you had me chop up was from the Cleveland Faction, right? They practically live on venom. I'm sure his bodily tissues are saturated with it."

He leans back on his toilet throne. I think I may have

satisfied him.

"Let me tell you a story," he says.

"I'd rather not. I've heard enough of your sermons," I say. This is no time to be snide, but I'm running out of anything to lose.

"This isn't a sermon. This is about my first years here. You know what I did? Me and some others killed a driver. We did it with this," he says, patting the shotgun like it's a faithful pet. "We drove the bus into the tunnel and barely made it back before running out of gas. The tunnel goes nowhere. Even with a bus, the tunnel goes nowhere."

"So what? Let me find out for myself. Let me kill a driver. You can spare a couple shotgun shells," I say.

"I'm not finished with the story. See, after we killed the driver, the buses dried up. They stopped coming. For two years, not a single bus," he says. "You think it's shitty here now? You should see it with no buses. No new supplies. No new citizens. Nothing. No hope at all. There were nearly two-hundred people here when we first killed the driver. After those two years, we were down to two-dozen. Everybody starved. Committed suicide. Killed each other. Ate each other." He pauses for some sort of dramatic effect. The effect is lost on me. I don't give a shit. I have stopped believing what he tells me. "I don't ever want to live through that again. What I do, I do for the good of the people. I do it to help us survive."

He lets the shotgun fall to his side, almost like he's comfortable with me again, like we've still got a peaceful arrangement. I consider my end-game. I wonder if I can hit him with my rock and just go for it. There are still guards nearby. I doubt I can get to the shotgun quickly enough. I take deep breaths. I consider the tally marks on the underside of my blouse. I have been here thirty-three days. I tell myself that I have time. I tell myself that I don't need to run headlong into a spray of bullets. I tell myself that I can collect more venom. I shout my rallying cry out loud: "I'm not dying today." I say it with gusto, but I do not believe the words anymore. I reel back and throw the rock at Chicago-Prophet. It thuds into his shoulder, and before I'm halfway to him, the shotgun rises and I'm staring down both barrels.

"That's what I thought," Chicago-Prophet says. The guards approach and they fasten some type of restraint on my leg. I think it's a bent bike lock. I can't be sure. "I'm done with this shit. I don't know why I haven't killed you yet," he says.

"Because you're scared," I sneer.

He leans in. Through gritted teeth, he says "You're scared too. I know it. You pretend like you're not, but you're terrified." He smashes the butt of the shotgun into my face. My nose splits open. The warm blood is almost soothing. The guards pull me from the hotel and take me back to my shanty. They drive a large stake-like piece of wood into the ground—the wood is strong and doesn't seem to be from the burnt forest. They fasten the other end of the twisted bike lock to the stake, tethering me like a dog. They walk over to the ravens and strangle each one.

I remember when my asshole husband strangled my big calico cat.

Toothless-Teen runs over and says "What are you doing to the birds! That wasn't part of the deal!" She's got new lipstick—pink this time. She starts crying. I scream at her. I tell her she's a traitor. I tell her she'll never be a good butcher. She runs away.

I touch my broken nose, and a blinding dizziness washes over me, like a migraine mixed with a hangover mixed with a tooth extraction. I think it's broken. I wipe away blood and mucus, but it doesn't stop. I take a dollop of Purell and rub it into my nostrils. It stings, but I hope it will ward off bacterial infection. Naked-Boy scampers over and grabs a glob of the mucus. Maybe Naked-Boy thinks it's some hunk of flesh that can be fried up as a treat. He'll be disappointed when he learns that it's just blood thickened with snot. Tarp-Woman calls him. I can't hear what she's saying, but I think she's telling him that he isn't allowed to come to my shanty anymore. I want to apologize for killing her boyfriend. I want to tell her that she's my best friend here. I want to tell her that I love her. But I do not say any of these things. Instead, I scream "fuck you" at the top of my lungs.

I take off my bra and tear the cottony cups into smaller pieces. I stuff some cotton fibers into my nose to stop the bleeding. I use an elastic piece of my bra strap to cover the outside of my nose. I tie it off, like a fucked up headband. The pressure keeps my nostrils from moving when I breathe. I'm sorry to see the bra go—it was the most comfortable one I ever owned, special ordered to compensate for my significantly smaller left breast.

The guards dump Condom-Eye's body in front of my shanty. They give me the cleaver, but they both stand there the entire time. They probably think I'm liable to cut off my foot and squirm away. But I honestly don't know what I'd do if I got free. Without Chicago-Prophet's gun, any plot to overtake the bus is a suicide mission. It's probably suicide even with a gun. It's always been that way. Every shitty escape attempt. Suicidal. Pointless. I wonder if I ever had a chance. I'm ready to die.

Chapter 14

The townspeople turn on me.

They forget my time in the tunnel.

They curse the Butcher Faction.

Tarp-Woman does not talk to me.

Neither does Naked-Boy.

Neither does Toothless-Teen.

Scarred-Back stays in his shanty.

Toothless-Teen has acquired two new ravens.

She raises the ravens by herself.

She does not wear makeup anymore.

Her mouth is full of blood.

It is her gums again.

Or her throat.

Or her stomach.

She spits.

She winches her usual wince.

She chops off rat heads.

She slides the knife across the rat sternums.

She cuts away slivers of sinew.

She sucks on the remains with her toothless gums.

There is so little meat on these bones.

These are rats.

Rats are insignificant.

They are not real, substantial, meaty livestock.

Just rats.

Rats.

Rats.

Toothless-Teen is getting better at this.

Chicago-Prophet won't need me soon.

Toothless-Teen slices her hand.

She pretends it's an accident.

She does not leave me any food.

I pull meat from my hidden stockpile in the cold mud.

Half of it is rancid.

I'm losing weight.

My ankle is smaller.

I twist my ankle and pop the joint.

I get out of the restraint fairly easily.

I have nowhere to go.

I slide the restraint back on.

My nose bleeds again.

A dirt storm rolls into Out of Service—stronger than any I've seen. It tests the tensile strength of my shanty. I curl into a tight ball, waiting for the storm to pass. Tarp-Woman donates her tarp to help shield a small cluster of townspeople. Others huddle near the hotel, using it as a giant windbreaker against horizontal gusts of filth. Some townies hold up a metal sheet near the fire barrel to make sure it doesn't extinguish. All across Out of Service, clumps of people hold tight and stay warm. Their dirty arms intertwine. Two townies kiss. I do not recognize them. I do not know these lovers, but I presume they hate me. A large piece of my shanty blows away. The dirty wind lashes my flesh with little airborne pebbles and coats me in a thick grime.

When the storm finally subsides, I strip down and use a daub of Purell to clean off the worst of it. I rub a little into my hair and a clump comes out. I mark the Purell level. I check the tally marks on my blouse. I try to remember if I tallied this morning. I wonder if there are other days when I forgot. Time is relative. I count forty tallies. Or should it be forty-one?

I sit in the middle of my empty hovel and consider taking the twisted hangers off my shanty. I look at my wrists. My old scars are still there. It would be so easy to slide the bent hanger right into that scar tissue, popping open a fresh wound. Fuck this place. I put my head in my hands. I scream something to myself. I don't even know what it is. It's not a word. It's just a sound. Something deep inside that I need to say, but I don't know how.

I pick up the Bush's Baked Beans can and wonder if there's any residue left. I lick the inside of the can, hoping it will take me far away from here.

Chapter 15

YOU ARE NOT YOU

Chapter 16

I hear the familiar low hiss of a bus stopping while Toothless-Teen and I cut some dead rats. My nose ruptures again while we work—it's been over a week and it still hasn't healed properly. I sop up some extra blood with my panties—I hope there isn't another dirt storm soon. Accordion doors open. Toothless-Teen smiles and says "Look!"

I do not say anything. I keep cutting.

"Look," she repeats.

I drop the paring knife and pick up the cleaver. These rats are already headless, so I don't need the cleaver, but I chop them anyway. I grunt and bring the cleaver downward with all my strength. I pulverize their tiny rat bodies and scream "Leave me alone!"

"But look at the destination!"

I turn. The bus marquee reads *Not in Service*. Not exactly a return trip to Seattle, but better than Out of Service. Anything is better than this shithole. Anything.

"Holy shit," I mutter. I throw the sopping, reddened panties at Toothless-Teen. I could put the cleaver through her skull, or I could kiss her. I could demand an apology, or I could offer one. I remember our talk—the only time I really talked to anybody here. The only time I didn't feel alone. The only time I said something nice and meant it. I think about her birds and her smile and her lipstick, and I say "We're leaving," and that's all it takes to mend the chasm. I know she will go with me. She wants to leave. She wants a new prophet.

I yank my foot from the bike lock. I don't even bother with the delicate joint-pop that I've perfected. I just yank as hard as I can. My heel scrapes apart and blood trickles across my foot. I don't even care. There's no way I'm missing this bus. I grab my Folgers tin with one hand, and I'm still holding the cleaver in my right.

I run through town and scream "Hold the doors!" Toothless-Teen is right behind me. I peak into Scarred-Back's shanty. For once, he's not actually there. I don't know where to find him, and I don't have time. Tarp-Woman is huddled around the fire with Naked-Boy, most likely cooking something in her hubcap. I don't even need to call out to her; she just looks at the marquee, then at me, and she shakes her head. That's fine by me. Let her stay. I tell myself she will live—she's been here long enough to know how to survive, even without Condom-Eye. I shout "I'm sorry," but I know it's too late. I know she does not forgive me, and I do not want her to. She holds Naked-Boy's hand and keeps him close. Naked-Boy waves goodbye with his wrist-nub. He's wearing those ruined Air Jordans. He will be okay.

I give New-Driver a big smile. It hurts. My gums bleed. "One ticket please." I give a handful of coins to New-Driver and set the Folgers tin down in the dirt. It probably contains enough money for four or five more fares. Toothless-Teen scoops out some change. She follows me aboard and there's an uproar. Other townspeople grab at the Folgers tin, and the change spills everywhere, most of it disappearing into the mud. A few people manage to get a couple coins.

"Blasphemy!" some townspeople scream. Others try to board but don't have enough change. They have been waiting for a prophesied bus—most of them for several years—but they never bothered to save any money for the fare. New-Driver stands behind the threshold with a double-barrel, big-ass sawed-off shotgun—just like Chicago-Prophet's—and nobody dares push onto the bus. Lights flicker in the hills. Any surviving members of the Cleveland Faction are probably waking from their spider venom stupors to see what's happening. Maybe they think their messiah bus has come. They won't make it to the bus in time.

I clutch the cleaver both hands. The mob is still respecting New-Driver's authority, not wanting to cross paths with his gun. I'm probably safe on-board, but I won't know for sure until the bus starts moving. I'm not giving up my seat for anything. Toothless-Teen runs her hands over the stained bus upholstery with its fuzzy neon pattern. She giggles. I think she's never felt a textile that wasn't slathered with mud before. She doesn't know that things can be soft.

Outside of the bus, Ass-Starer gets on top of a mound of dirt and begins to wave his hands. I wonder what that little shit is doing now. He tries to calm the crowd. "This is not the bus that was foretold to us by the great prophet. This is not the bus to Chicago. This is just a temptation sent by evil doers. This is

127

not the path to salvation. All praise Chicago!"

On cue, Chicago-Prophet weaves through the crowd and everybody shuts up, expecting a sermon. Ass-Starer even stops his rant in anticipation of the prophet's wisdom. Chicago-Prophet looks at the marquee, throws down his shotgun, reaches into his coonskin cloak, and retrieves exact change for the bus. As he boards, Ass-Starer picks up the gun and points it at Chicago-Prophet's back. The big-ass gun makes a click. There are no shells. The chamber has probably been empty for years.

Ass-Starer tosses aside the gun and rushes the bus with his broken Miller Lite bottle. He screams something about betrayal or blasphemy or some other bullshit. New-Driver's big ass gun has bullets. Blood sprays the crowd. One person screams, a couple others cry, most don't flinch.

Chicago-Prophet moves toward the back of the bus. On his way, he bends over and picks up a bit of garbage from the bus floor. I raise the cleaver, still gripping with both hands, not sure what to expect of Chicago-Prophet. He sits next to me and sighs. New-Driver closes the door, and we begin a slow departure.

Toothless-Teen is still inspecting the seats. She finds what appears to be a soda stain. She begins licking it. Chicago-Prophet holds out the bit of garbage. I put away the cleaver and take the weathered piece of cardboard from him. On one side are cooking directions for a DiGiorno pepperoni pizza. On the backside it reads *Can I please leave?* in my handwriting. I laugh. This isn't even the same bus. There's no red splotch near the door.

The bus starts to rock as the townspeople push against it. New-Driver speeds up and runs over a few people. "If you had killed me, you would've made a really good prophet," Chicago-Prophet tells me. He pulls some raccoon meat from his pocket and offers me a tear.

"I never wanted to be a prophet," I explain. I take a piece and pop it in my mouth. It's chewy like a gumball—probably a piece of cartilage.

"Neither did I," Chicago-Prophet says.

"What's your name?" I ask.

He tells me and shakes my hand. It's an even more generic name than I expect. Donald Williamson, or William Donaldson, or some bullshit like that. He might as well be my next door neighbor, or customer number thirty-two at the deli, or any random person on my daily commute. The bus jostles around again, inconvenienced by more human speed bumps. Toothless-Teen grabs hold of a nearby railing and swings into the seat in front of us. She reaches into the front pocket of her tattered pants. She pulls out that gaudy red lipstick. It doesn't smudge this time. She smiles at me. We enter the black-hole-esque tunnel bound for Not in Service, and I have never been happier.

Acknowledgements

Thank you, Uma Sankaram, for being one of the strongest and most resilient women I know. Ren Powell for feedback on this story and so many others. Etchings Press and the University of Indianapolis for believing in small books. Finally, special thanks to bus drivers everywhere.

James R. Gapinski's collection of linked flashes, *Messiah Tortoise*, is available from Red Bird Chapbooks. His work has also appeared in *The Collapsar*, *F(r)iction*, *Juked*, *Monkeybicycle*, *Paper Darts*, *Psychopomp*, and other publications. He's managing editor of *The Conium Review*, associate faculty at Ashford University, and an instructional specialist at Chemeketa Community College. James is originally from southeastern Wisconsin. He now lives with his partner in Portland, Oregon.

Etchings Press Chapbook and Novella Contests

Etchings Press, a student-run publisher at the University of Indianapolis, invites submissions for its annual chapbook contest. Chapbook submissions in poetry, short fiction or nonfiction, and novella submissions will be accepted. The winners receive a cash prize and 15 author copies of their published book.

Please review guidelines and submit chapbook and novella manuscripts at etchings.submittable.com. Submission deadlines fall in January each year.

For more information, please visit blogs.unidy.edu/etchings or email uindyetchings@gmail.com.